"I'm a bee," a voice hissed in the darkness. "I want to pollinate you. I'd like to lift your petals."

The startled Mrs. Pasquith froze in terror. There was no doubt about it. The same person who had molested Brangwyn Butters and Brenda Sweeting now had her cornered in the empty church. Inspector Purbright and his assistants were nowhere to be seen. She would have to escape by her own wits. If only she could reach the vestry. The sinister breathing was coming closer and closer. She made a desperate dash for the door....

Murder Ink.® Mysteries

1. DEATH IN THE MORNING, Sheila Radley
3. THE BRANDERBURG HOTEL, Pauline Glen Winslow
5. McGARR AND THE SIENESE CONSPIRACY, Bartholomew Gill
7. THE RED HOUSE MYSTERY, A.A. Milne
9. THE MINUTEMAN MURDERS, Jane Langton
11. MY FOE OUTSTRETCH'D BENEATH THE TREE, V.C. Clinton-Baddeley
13. GUILT EDGED, W.J. Burley
15. COPPER GOLD, Pauline Glen Winslow
17. MANY DEADLY RETURNS, Patricia Moyes
19. McGARR AT THE DUBLIN HORSE SHOW, Bartholomew Gill
21. DEATH AND LETTERS, Elizabeth Daly
23. ONLY A MATTER OF TIME, V.C. Clinton-Baddeley
25. WYCLIFFE AND THE PEA-GREEN BOAT, W.J. Burley
27. ANY SHAPE OR FORM, Elizabeth Daly
29. COFFIN SCARCELY USED, Colin Watson
31. THE CHIEF INSPECTOR'S DAUGHTER, Sheila Radley
33. PREMEDICATED MURDER, Douglas Clark
35. NO CASE FOR THE POLICE, V.C. Clinton-Baddeley
37. JUST WHAT THE DOCTOR ORDERED, Colin Watson

Scene Of The Crime ™ Mysteries

2. A MEDIUM FOR MURDER, Mignon Warner
4. DEATH OF A MYSTERY WRITER, Robert Barnard
6. DEATH AFTER BREAKFAST, Hugh Pentecost
8. THE POISONED CHOCOLATES CASE, Anthony Berkeley
10. A SPRIG OF SEA LAVENDER, J.R.L. Anderson
12. WATSON'S CHOICE, Gladys Mitchell
14. SPENCE AND THE HOLIDAY MURDERS, Michael Allen
16. THE TAROT MURDERS, Mignon Warner
18. DEATH ON THE HIGH C'S, Robert Barnard
20. WINKING AT THE BRIM, Gladys Mitchell
22. TRIAL AND ERROR, Anthony Berkeley
24. RANDOM KILLER, Hugh Pentecost
26. SPENCE AT THE BLUE BAZAAR, Michael Allen
28. GENTLY WITH THE INNOCENTS, Alan Hunter
30. THE JUDAS PAIR, Jonathan Gash
32. DEATH OF A LITERARY WIDOW, Robert Barnard
34. THE TWELVE DEATHS OF CHRISTMAS, Marian Babson
36. GOLD BY GEMINI, Jonathan Gash
38. LANDED GENTLY, Alan Hunter

A Murder Ink.® Mystery

JUST WHAT THE DOCTOR ORDERED

formerly titled
The Flaxborough Crab

Colin Watson

A DELL BOOK

Published by
Dell Publishing Co., Inc.
1 Dag Hammarskjold Plaza
New York, New York 10017

This work was first published in Great Britain
under the title THE FLAXBOROUGH CRAB.

ISBN: 0-440-14242-3

Reprinted by arrangement with the author
Printed in the United States of America
First Dell printing—February 1982

CHAPTER ONE

Miss Brangwyn Butters, Flaxborough's Assistant Librarian, was thirty-six years old. She was healthy and had been described more than once as handsome. No one had ever declared her pretty. This did not worry her at all. She did not despise beauty, but she recognized that it could be more of a nuisance than an asset. From what she had heard of the conversation of the younger girls in her charge at the municipal library, it was clear that their concern with their good looks and with the attention they drew was by no means an entirely happy state of mind. Miss Butters saw nothing to be envied in a preoccupation with weighing machines and tape measures. Nor did she feel any sense of loss in being unable to share in that vapid, fragmentary, apparently endless discussion of cosmetics and fashion which was the girls' sole intellectual exercise. The truth was, she told herself that underneath their preening and chatter they were afraid.

Miss Butters was not afraid of anything. She certainly was not apprehensive of being raped: that particular fantasy she considered to be the prerogative of the pretty and the bird-brained.

Which is why she never hesitated in her habit of taking a walk every Tuesday and Friday evening along the riverside as far as Hoare's Sluice and back through Gorry Wood.

One Tuesday at dusk, Miss Butters had just completed the three seaward miles from Flaxborough along the top of the river embankment and was about to descend to the road and the stile leading to the return path through the wood, when she noticed two objects in the water. They were dark and round and looked like a pair of half-submerged footballs. The naturalist in Miss Butters was delightedly aroused.

She waited, hoping that the seals would swim closer and even emerge on the mud below, but they kept to their business-like course in mid-stream and in about ten minutes she lost sight of them.

Would there be others? She had heard of these occasional incursions from the estuary, where several dozen seals could sometimes be seen sunning themselves on the mudflats, but they were rare. She decided that expectation of a second stroke of luck in one evening would be quite unreasonable. If Miss Butters was not a fearful woman, neither was she an over-sanguine one.

By the time she reached Gorry Wood, it was later and therefore darker than she had envisaged on setting out. There was no question of getting lost or of bumping into obstacles—she was familiar with every turn and dip of the path—but she realized that it would be sensible to abandon her original intention of rooting up some bluebell bulbs for planting in her garden at home.

In her sturdy, flat-heeled shoes, she strode quickly and purposefully towards the black centre of the wood. The air was much colder here: it seemed to have been left behind by winter, together with the pungent mulch of dead leaves and the wet, black twigs. Miss Butters did not mind the cold. Her brisk, healthy circulation was proof against it. She did not mind the smell of decay. All "natural" smells pleased her, and some—including that of mushrooms—fascinated her. Reaching a spot where she knew a great yellow shelf of fungus jutted from a dead tree trunk, she paused and sniffed appreciatively.

It was at that moment, when the noise of her own footfalls was stilled, that she knew she was not alone in the wood.

Someone—manifestly neither bird nor animal—coughed.

It was suppressed, a sort of concert hall cough, and there followed a quick intake of breath as though the attempt to smother it had been something of a strain.

Miss Butters remained absolutely still, trying to fix the source of the sound. Whoever had made it was undoubtedly close at hand, but the cloistral enclosure of the trees made it difficult to decide in which direction.

She waited, frowning in the dark. Whatever sense of danger stirred in her was speculative rather than cowering. Who was this person? Was he authorized or an intruder? And what on earth did he hope to gain by creeping around in a wood where it was too dark even to dig bluebell bulbs?

The possibility of an impending attack upon herself simply did not occur to her.

But of course it came.

There was a sudden rustle of undergrowth, a squelch of feet in the wet leaves behind her, and, almost in her ear, a cry like the whinny of a winded horse.

Before she could turn, an arm snaked round her waist from behind. It tightened in an effort to throw her to the ground.

Miss Butters allowed no such thing to happen. She

stood firm and, having concluded that her handbag was the object of the attack, she transferred it from her left hand to the greater safety of her right. She then glanced down to assess the nature of her assailant.

He had stooped low to put the maximum leverage against her middle—somewhat in the fashion of an American football tackle—and his head was now pressed against her left side. He was breathing rather heavily. Miss Butters was sorry about that, but she was also determined not to part with her handbag, which contained a set of the library keys, a small gardening fork, fifteen shillings, and an eight years old powder compact, in that order of importance. So she did the obvious thing and scissored the man's head between her waist and her left arm.

He was thus under effective arrest. Miss Butters considered what she should do next.

A decision was not easy. It would be unwise to lay herself open to further violence by relinquishing her hold. The man might have a weapon. And if he did not, there were plenty of pieces of timber lying around from which he could improvise one.

She could, of course, try and march him as he was to some house at which help might be enlisted. The nearest she could think of, though, was at least half a mile away. Half a mile would seem a terribly long journey with so reluctant a travelling companion; already he had managed to twist his head round a few inches and was trying to bite her arm.

Miss Butters twisted the head back again and tightened her lock upon it. She sighed.

'I'm sorry,' she said to the head.

Afterwards she was to reflect that these had been the only words spoken by either of them during the entire encounter. At the time, they seemed apposite enough. They expressed her genuine regret before she stepped resolutely to the handiest tree and rammed the captive cranium against it twice, then once again for good measure.

The man cried out each time, but the third yell was much weaker than the first. Miss Butters concluded that the security of her handbag was no longer in doubt. She released her grip on the man's neck and prepared to demand that he identify himself and give an account of his behaviour.

He staggered a little away from her and remained stooped, his head averted, while he recovered his breath.

Miss Butters charitably allowed him a whole minute for this purpose. It was a mistake. At her sternly boomed 'Well?' the man launched himself into flight with such suddenness and vigour that the stolidly built Miss Butters knew that pursuit would be not only undignified but almost certainly useless.

She watched him career back along the path towards the river road, an amorphous shape that soon merged with the darkness.

There was one thing about his mode of escape which much intrigued her. After his first five or six paces of fairly straightforward sprinting, he appeared to turn through ninety degrees and yet fully to maintain speed, even in that highly unconventional relationship to the axis of his escape route, by a series of sideways leaps and scuttles.

He runs like a scalded crab, reflected Miss Butters. How very queer.

The rest of her walk was uneventful and she spent the half hour it took her to reach the lighted streets of Flaxborough in mental formulation of a lucid and practical report of her experience. That was what the police would expect, and that was what she, a conscientious citizen, would give them.

It did not occur to Miss Butters, as it might have done to a more timid or more devious woman, to avoid by silence the inconvenience and distress of involvement in a criminal inquiry. Assailants in woods were, to her mind, in exactly the same category as gas leaks and unfenced pits and maltreated horses. Dealing with them was what Authority existed for.

She tapped firmly on the "Inquiries" window just inside the entrance to the Fen Street police station.

The window was slid up noisily by a rather surprised-looking young constable. The top four of his uniform buttons were undone. He gave the impression of a householder getting ready for bed.

'I wish to report having been accosted by a footpad,' Miss Butters announced.

The policeman wrinkled his nose—not very attractively, thought Miss Butters—and said: 'You what?'

'I have been accosted. I wish to report it.'

The constable stared at her dubiously for some seconds, then rubbed his jaw with one hand and with the other dragged nearer an enormous ledger on the shelf beneath the window.

'Name?'

'Butters. Miss Brangwyn Butters.'

She spelled this out for him while he wrote it in one of the columns of the ledger. He had all the dash of a monumental mason with arthritis.

'Age?'

She told him. He began the task of recording her address. The night was young.

'Now then,' he said at last, 'what's this you said happened?'

Miss Butters sighed. 'I told you I'd been accosted. In Gorry Wood. By a footpad.'

The constable stared at her. 'A what?'

'A footpad. I can't think of any other way to describe him. A footpad is somebody who lies in wait to rob people.'

'Never heard of it.'

'In that case, you are very ignorant. It is a perfectly ordinary dictionary word.' The constable looked a little hurt. She relented. 'Like highwayman, you know. Only without a horse.'

'Ah, he hadn't a horse, this . . . what was it you called him?'

Miss Butters was very nearly at the end of her patience. 'We'll just call him a man, shall we? Then perhaps we shall waste no more time. I am late home already and my mother will be getting anxious. All I ask is . . .'

A shadow fell across the open pages of the report book.

'Is there anything I could do to help this lady, Mr Braine?'

A tall, very fair-haired man in civilian clothes had arrived to tower (rather god-like, Miss Butters thought) over the constable's shoulder. She gave him a small, grateful smile.

The uniformed man moved respectfully aside and indicated what he had written so far. 'She says she's been having some trouble with'—his glance flickered disbelievingly to Miss Butters—'what she calls a footpad. Is that right, madam?'

Miss Butters nodded. (Braine, she was thinking—no, surely too good to be true.)

Into the tall man's benignly watchful eye came sudden concern. 'You've been attacked?'

'Yes, I suppose I have.'

At once he was at the door of the office, beckoning her in, taking her arm. He gave her Constable Braine's chair and sent its late occupant to fetch her a cup of tea from the canteen.

'You're not hurt?'

'No, oh no, he didn't actually hurt me. Rather the other way round.' She permitted herself a tiny nibble at the sin of pride.

'I am glad to hear it. My name, by the way, is Purbright. Detective Inspector.'

'Oh, yes, I know. You are the only policeman who comes into the library. Except for Mr Chubb, of course, but he only collects books for his wife. She seems to have a very lurid taste.'

Purbright loyally refrained from exposing what he knew to be the Chief Constable's duplicity: Mrs Chubb had not read a book for years.

'What I propose,' he said, 'is to send a couple of my men to take a look round the area where you were attacked. It is very unlikely that the man is still there but there is always the chance that he has waited in hope of a less formidable victim. Do you think you can manage a description?'

Miss Butters looked regretful. 'The funny thing is that I never got a look at his face. It was fairly dark, of course, in the wood, and he came on me from behind. That's how I managed to catch his head under my arm. I held it there and gave it one or two whacks against a tree trunk.'

'Did you, indeed?'

'Yes. It was rather vicious of me, I suppose, but I couldn't think of any other way of calming him down.'

'He was excited, was he?'

'Decidedly.'

'Why did he attack you, do you think, Miss Butters?'

'Well, to get my handbag, naturally. What other reason could he have?'

Purbright forebore from naming the more cogent motive. 'Did you get any impression of his age?'

'Certainly not young. Past middle age, I should say. There was a sort of brittle, bony feel about him. And he wheezed.'

'Did you notice his hair?'

'Only that it seemed pretty thin.'

'Height?'

'A bit shorter than me, I think—about five feet six or seven.'

'What about clothing?'

'He was wearing a coat, grey or light brown. It was rather loose and flappy—thin, a sort of raincoat, I should say. No hat.'

Braine entered with short, careful steps. He was carrying a cup of tea as if it were a delicately fused bomb. When he had delivered it into Miss Butters' lap, Purbright sent him off again to summon the two-man crew of a patrol car that had just driven past the window into the station yard.

Constables Fairclough and Brevitt presented themselves two minutes later. Fairclough was a fat, breezy man who looked capable of giving good account of himself in a chase, provided he did not actually have to get out of the car. That, obviously, would be the role of the correspondingly lean Brevitt, who stood listening to the inspector's instructions with one eye on the door as if it were a race track starting gate.

'You'll just have to circle round that area for a while,' Purbright was saying, 'and watch out for the sort of fellow I've described. If you do spot a likely character—which I might say is highly unlikely—there is probably only one way in which suspicion can be confirmed. The odds are that the man we're looking for has a lump on the top of his head.'

Fairclough looked cheerful but unenlightened. Brevitt, on the other hand, gave a determined nod of comprehension. If everything depended on a lump, his expression implied, so small a matter could be very easily arranged.

'Of course,' Purbright added, 'I don't need to remind such experienced officers as yourselves that the utmost tact must be employed. People don't much like being stopped late at night by policemen eager to practise phrenology.'

The two patrolmen smiled, one amiably, the other darkly at his own thoughts.

As the inspector had predicted, exploration of the Gorry Wood neighborhood was unproductive. A light rain had begun to fall and the lanes were empty and miserable in the slow advance of the headlights. The policemen's only encounter, other than with an occasional zig-zagging hare, was their discovery of the Vicar of Pitney leaning over the rectory gate and flagging them down with an empty beer bottle. 'I'm sorry, I thought you were the butcher,' he had said, before tottering indoors again. Brevitt was at first for pursuit and forcible bump-reading, but he deferred to his colleague's opinion that such a course would be trespass, if not sacrilege.

Miss Butters remained at the police station long enough to finish her tea and to add to her account a point that she said she was sorry not to have remembered in time for it to serve as further guidance to the officers who had gone in search of her assailant.

'It was the way he ran,' she said. 'I've never seen anything quite like it before. You know how soldiers shuffle along to one side when they are doing drill—closing ranks, do they call it? Anyway, it was rather like that, only much, much faster and with bigger steps, of course. He was actually running sideways, if you can imagine such a thing.'

'What, like a crab?'

'That's it exactly. Like a crab. Now isn't that odd?'

'Most decidedly,' said Purbright.

CHAPTER TWO

Unlike Miss Butters, nineteen years old Brenda Sweeting, shop assistant, considered sexual molestation to be a permanent and universal hazard.

This view derived partly from her mother's admonition, repeated every day in life, to 'watch your step and mind who you talk to'; partly from a certain freedom of gesture and remark that characterized the young Flaxborough male; but chiefly from the traumatic experience in early childhood of hearing auntie command: 'Don't pick those flowers, dear: the dicky-birds have wee-wee'd on them.'

In a world where even birds had villainous habits and the very flowers were impure, it was obvious to Brenda that merely human virginity was at a pretty sharp discount.

She knew what to expect, therefore, when an arm reached out from a bush-enshrouded driveway on Heston Lane and closed round her waist.

The time was half-past ten and Brenda was on her way home after spending the evening with a girl friend. Heston Lane was not the shortest route she could have chosen, but it was the best lighted and an occasional bus passed along it. Moreover, the Heston Lane residents were reputed to be of good financial standing, and this quality was naively equated in Brenda's mind with aloofness from lust.

Almost before the arm touched her, she screamed. The scream had been on a hair trigger, so to speak, and it went off at full charge. She twisted, tugged, flailed and kicked. Then she screamed again. But the arm held fast.

Not a door opened in Heston Lane. Those occupants who heard Brenda's cries were accustomed, unfortunately for her, to associating such sounds with the boisterous enjoyment of the lower classes. They winced disapprovingly, and hoped the rhododendrons were not taking too bad a beating.

The point at which Brenda had been waylaid was exactly midway between two street lamps and fairly dark in consequence but she managed to resist the man's efforts to drag her into the even deeper obscurity of the driveway from which he had emerged.

A third scream brought no sign of rescue, so she concentrated her energy into wrenching herself nearer the light. Kicks were now more painful to her than to their target, as both shoes had fallen off, so she used her knees instead.

One luckily placed blow earned a sharp wail of distress and she gained another three yards towards the lamp. But still she could not break free of the encircling arm.

With his other hand the man was warding off the punches that Brenda repeatedly but not very effectually directed towards his lowered, always averted, face. At last he caught and held her wrist.

His grip on her flesh was dry and bony. It frightened her more than anything else that had happened to her so far. She knew that the grip was not very strong. Yet she could not tug her wrist away. The sudden revelation of her own spent strength was a horror that buckled her and laid her sobbing and slack across the arm she had been fighting to escape.

The man stood there, hesitant. He seemed bewildered by the collapse of the girl's resistance. Several seconds went by before he started, his attention caught by the approach of a car from the direction of the town.

He grasped Brenda close in both arms and began half-carrying, half-dragging her back to the driveway.

The car, travelling fast, was only two or three hundred yards distant. The note of its engine changed. Brenda felt her captor's effort increase. He was taking great gulps of breath as he heaved her like a too-heavy sack. The twigs of a bush raked across her face.

It was only then that the noise of the car broke into her consciousness. She opened her eyes a little. The hot, thick tears transmuted the headlamps' glare into a jumbled constellation of bright silver orbs, but she knew that they signified the possibility of deliverance. She strained towards the light and threw into it one last retching scream.

She was alone, free of the grappling, claw-like hands and of the rasping breath that had smelled unpleasantly of cigarette-ends and cough medicine. She knelt, head bowed, and was grateful for the feel of cold asphalt through her torn stockings.

Somewhere a car door slammed. There was a shout, a scuffling of feet.

Brenda looked about her wonderingly.

The car, its lights still ablaze, was across the pavement a few yards away, angled ready to enter the drive of one of the houses. Running away from the car were two men, pursued and pursuer. Brenda watched them cross the road and pass through the pool of light cast by the nearest street lamp.

She thought the first man was going to fall over. He had turned as he ran and was now scuttling along sideways, his legs all over the place.

The girl giggled, then at once began to cry again. She saw one of her shoes lying in the road. She bent over and picked it up.

When she caught sight of the two men again, they were almost directly beneath the next street lamp. One had grabbed the other's arm and was pulling him to a halt. Brenda felt pleased that her attacker had been caught. Now he would be punished. At the same time, her terror was renewed at the thought of having him once again in close proximity, even under the guard of policemen.

She turned away and limped painfully towards the car, searching the ground for her other shoe. When she found it, she saw with a new stab of distress that it was broken, ruined. She thought of the impending disapproval of her mother and hated the old man even more.

Old. That he *was* old, it had not occurred to her to doubt. He had felt and smelled old. The girl shuddered and carefully eased on the broken shoe while she supported herself against the car.

Someone was crossing the road towards her. She looked up. The owner of the car, the old man's pursuer. But he was alone.

'Now, young lady.'

He was a man she had seen before several times, here and there in the town; tall, quite handsome, self-possessed; not young, though. He looked well off.

Her gaze slipped past him into the dark and became a stare of alarm.

'Where is he?'

The man shrugged elegantly. 'I'm afraid he got away.' He saw her expression. 'You're quite safe now, though. Don't worry. Just let me take the car in and we'll have a look at you in the house.'

She knew now who he was. Doctor Meadow. Quite a posh doctor. Her friend Sylvia Bart was one of his patients. Yes, but . . .

'But he can't have! That old man. Got away, I mean. You had hold of him.'

'I'm afraid he did, though. Look—keep close to the car and I'll see you at the front door. Then I'll drive you home again afterwards.'

The house was very grand. As the doctor led her through a panelled hall with thick carpet on the floor, he switched on one light after another and left them burning even after they had passed into a side room and through that to a much bigger one with long crimson velvet curtains draping a window the size of a cinema screen. In this room, Brenda counted eight separate lamps. Five were set in the walls behind pink silk shades, gold-braided. The other three were huge standard lamps, taller than herself. Her feet sank into carpet as thick as a sheep's fleece and of the colour of very milky coffee. The four armchairs and two settees were every bit as splendid looking, in their livery of pale cerise damask, as those in the new Odeon foyer had been when it was first re-opened for Bingo.

The doctor led her gently to one of the chairs and stood looking down at her. He held her wrist for a few seconds, very lightly, then stooped to peer at her eyes. She caught a faint smell, not unpleasant, that was half-way between scent and disinfectant. As he examined her, Meadow hummed behind a wide but handsome mouth. Brenda thought he looked as if he shaved a lot:

the tanned skin was so smooth that it reflected the light of the standard lamp behind her.

"Mmm, hmm,' said Meadow, wisely. He rubbed long, white, well-washed hands, and nodded. 'Mm, hm.'

Brenda supposed this to signify that she had suffered no lasting harm.

'Hadn't you better ring up, now?' she asked, anxiously.

'Ring up?' Meadow had turned his attention to a small pile of letters lying on a scalloped walnut table nearby.

'The police.'

'Ah,' said Meadow to the envelope on the top of the pile. He clearly was a man capable of thinking of two or three things at once. Brenda waited for him to go over to the pale pink telephone that she had spotted on a beautifully polished writing desk near the window.

He did, in fact, stroll over to the desk, opening his letter as he moved; but when he reached it, it was to pull out a little drawer. He came back with a phial in his hand, shook a white tablet on to the table, and wordlessly invited her to swallow it. The tablet looked and tasted like aspirin.

When it had gone down, not without difficulty, the girl said: 'They could still catch him if you get on to them straight away.'

'Now, now—you mustn't worry.' He was reading the letter, not looking at her.

She shifted to the edge of the chair, as if about to get up.

'Would you rather I telephoned? I don't mind. The only trouble is, I can't tell them what he looks like, and you can.'

Meadow laid aside his correspondence and gave her a big concerned smile.

'Now, what *is* all this you're bothered about, eh?'

He had a fruity, very nicely educated voice, she thought; surely he couldn't be as thick as he pretended.

'The patient is our main concern, isn't she? How is she feeling now, hmm?' He felt her forehead with the backs of his fingers and pouted judiciously.

'I'm very much better, thank you, and I would like you to telephone the police at once.'

He laughed and walked to the phone.

She heard him give the policeman at the other end of the line the bare facts of what had happened. It did not sound a very exciting account. Then, after a pause, he called out: 'I say . . .' and she looked across to see him with his hand over the mouthpiece.

'They want to know your name and address.'

She told him. He repeated the words to his listener, enunciating them very clearly and with a faint smile as if there were something funny about being called Sweeting and living in Washington Road.

When he had put down the receiver, Meadow resumed reading his mail.

'They want you to stay here,' he told Brenda. 'It seems that someone is coming round to ask you some questions.'

'But I can't. Mum will be worrying her head off.'

'That's all right: they're letting your people know.' He had not looked up.

The girl continued to sit on the edge of her chair. She ruefully examined her holed stockings and twisted one foot to look at the damaged shoe. Then she noticed that a seam in her dress had been pulled apart. She tried to close the gap through which white nylon was showing.

The doctor, who had slipped the wrapper from a medical journal, was now leafing through it, apparently oblivious to her presence.

Five minutes went by. The girl sat hugging her knees and staring out through the big window. There was nothing to see but the trailing branch of a willow tree a few feet beyond the glass.

Suddenly she was aware of someone standing in the doorway. She turned.

A woman in an olive-green tweed suit was gazing at her with an expression compounded of inquiry and distaste. The woman was middle-aged and had a long, rather weather-beaten face. She looked energetic and determined to be neither persuaded nor amused by anyone on earth.

Her husband unhurriedly put down his magazine.

'This young lady,' he informed her, 'has had a rather nasty experience.'

Mrs Meadow's unchanged stare indicated her opinion that Brenda belonged to that group of young females for whom unpleasant experiences were customary nutriment.

'She is just having a little rest,' Meadow added, 'until the police arrive.'

'The police!'

'Some fellow attacked her in the road outside here. They will want to ask her some questions.'

'Is there any reason why she can't go to the police station? I mean, that is the usual procedure, isn't it?' Mrs Meadow had entered the room and was searching for something in the drawer of a glass-fronted bureau.

'Mmm?' said the doctor. The medical journal was engrossing him once more.

Brenda felt very guilty at having disturbed the routine of two such busy and important people. She remembered now having seen frequent references in the *Flaxborough Citizen* to Mrs Meadow's activities. She belonged to lots of things and was never photographed, indoors or out, without a hat—a sure sign of considerable social status.

The girl was about to suggest that perhaps she should go home now and call at the police station the next day, when she heard the mellifluous chimes of the Meadows' three-tone front door bell.

No one made a move. Then Mrs Meadow murmured something over her shoulder about being Elizabeth's night off. The doctor, still reading, strolled slowly out of the room.

He returned with two men.

One was Inspector Purbright.

The other was an individual whose patently mature bodily development was quite disconcertingly at odds with the face of a fourteen-year-old choir boy. This was Detective Sergeant Love, sometimes playfully referred to by his superiors as "whited-sepulchre Sid".

Mrs Meadow acknowledged introductions with only the slightest tilt of the boulder of her face. The ordained role of the police, she considered, was the protection of private property; if young women insisted on indulging in the frivolity of getting raped, then that was no good reason for the diversion of the constabulary from its proper duties.

It was with Brenda, now pale and weary-looking, that Purbright concerned himself at once.

He glanced at the table beside her.

'Have you had something to drink?'

'I have given her a sedative,' Meadow said.

'Oh, but a hot drink . . .' The inspector looked

across at Mrs Meadow. 'Do you think something in that line could be managed? Tea, perhaps?'

Mrs Meadow was too surprised to produce indignation commensurate with the audacity of the request. 'Well, it *is* rather awkward, actually. The maid . . .'

'No, no,' Purbright protested cheerfully. 'The sergeant is awfully good at making tea. He'd be pleased to do it.'

Love beamed like a boy scout unexpectedly invited to demonstrate fire-craft in the middle of the sitting-room carpet.

'I don't think that will be necessary,' said Mrs Meadow, already on her way to the door.

The sergeant took out his notebook and Purbright began asking Brenda quiet, gently phrased questions.

Dr Meadow listened.

CHAPTER THREE

The inspector and the sergeant discussed the ordeal of Miss Sweeting.

It was the following morning.

As in the case of the attack upon the resourceful librarian, the search for the man responsible had been undertaken more as a gesture of helpfulness than with any hope of success. It had been quite fruitless. Heston Lane could have been as uninhabited as Gorry Wood for all the notice its sequestered residents had taken of the drama in their midst.

One thing was clear. Both incidents displayed common features. And the most striking of these was the curious crab-like flight of the women's assailant.

'He's not one of the regulars, you know, Sid,' Purbright observed thoughtfully. He had been perusing the Flaxborough version of that list kept by every police force of its sexually enterprising locals, both the convicted and the so far lucky.

Love agreed.

'And yet,' the inspector went on, 'the girl and the Butters woman both speak of his being fairly old. Unless he's a new arrival in the district, it's queer that he should suddenly break out like this so late in life. These people are usually pretty well set in their ways.'

'Maybe it's the weather,' suggested the sergeant. 'They tell me they've had quite a bit of awkwardness over at Twilight Court during the past couple of weeks. They've cut out stout at supper on the men's wards.'

'They blamed water fluoridization last time.'

Love thought some more, then said: 'It's a pity the doctor didn't get a look at the bloke's face.'

'It's an even greater pity that he didn't hang on to him. If we are to believe the girl, he actually had hold of his arm when she saw them together under the lamp.'

Love looked at his notes. 'That's right,' he said. 'He did.'

'Meadow strikes me as being a reasonably fit man. I gather he goes in for winter sports. He used to row, too. I should have thought he'd have enough muscle to stop that old goat getting away, particularly when he was already winded through struggling with the girl.'

The sergeant was not so sure in his own mind of the validity of this argument. He had been brought up to hold the medical profession in awe, with the possible exception of pathologists (a queer, jokey lot) and police surgeons, who tended to be shabby and remote. A family practitioner, of all people, could not fairly be expected to put his dignity at hazard by tussling with felons.

'And why,' persisted Purbright, 'did Meadow claim not to have seen the man's face? The girl said he must have done. They were close together, directly under a lamp.'

'She couldn't have been certain that the doctor actually looked at him.'

'I'm inclined to think that he simply didn't want to become involved. That's why he let the fellow go, and that's why he now says he can't identify him. Another thing . . .'

Love waited stiffly to hear what new heresy had occurred to the inspector.

'Why did he wait so long before ringing us up? He let ten minutes or quarter of an hour go by. To say, as he did, that his first concern was for his patient just isn't good enough. Anyway, it was only on her insistence that he telephoned in the end.'

There was a pause. Then the sergeant inquired what was proposed to be done next. He sounded sulky. Late nights did not suit him, especially when his being summoned to an extra turn of duty conflicted with his landlady's almost religious observance of the household bath rota.

'Nothing we *can* do,' said Purbright. 'Our only hope is that next time this character performs there'll be on hand some less circumspect citizen than Dr Meadow.'

Three days went by before this hope was put to the test.

The victim, a Mrs Pasquith, was more fortunate than the previous two in as much as the assault was vocal and not physical. She was sufficiently distressed by it, however, to call at the police station twelve hours later and volunteer an account—on condition that the listener was a woman.

Mrs Pasquith was thereupon closeted with a brawny but soft-hearted policewoman called Sadie Bellweather.

'Well, you see, love,' Mrs Pasquith cozily began, 'I'm on vases and brasses this week at St Hilda's and last night I thought, well, I've got time before Harry comes back for his supper to go down and see to the flowers and bring the altar cloth home ready for taking to the launderette, well, I'd made a nice show of the gladioli on that side near the vestry door and I was just getting some fern together to go with the carnations from Harry's allotment when I hear this voice from somewhere at the back, well, I nearly jumped out of my skin but then straight away I thought it must be the vicar or Mr Hardy perhaps and I said hello, you know, without turning round, well . . . and then in a little while the voice came again, and this time I knew it wasn't the vicar because he said, "I'm a bee". Yes, that's what he said—"I'm a bee"—quite loud, well . . . I turned round and looked but I couldn't see anybody, of course it's very dark at the back there, well, I called out "Who's there?" and whoever it was called back, "I want to pollinate you". Well, what a funny thing to say. I didn't know what to make of it—well, *you* wouldn't, would you?—but then he made his voice go quite nasty and he said, "I'd like to lift your petals". Well! I knew then the sort of thing he was hinting at—wouldn't *you* have done?—and I thought, right, don't you come any nearer . . .'

'Could you,' interposed Policewoman Bellweather, 'see nothing at all of this man?'

Mrs Pasquith tightened her motherly, quilt-like features and leaned nearer. 'Not his face, I couldn't. He was just a sort of dark shadow, but I think'—her voice switched dramatically to a whisper—'that he was playing with himself!'

The big, sympathetic face of Policewoman Bellweather bobbed slightly in acknowledgment of this not unexpected circumstance. Most of the cases that came her way seemed to be concerned with the more bizarre manifestations of male vanity.

'Anyway,' continued Mrs Pasquith in her normal tone, 'I pretended not to have heard—that's usually the best way to deal with people like that—but I picked up a vase just in case and began moving nearer the vestry door, well, there's a telephone in there and you can lock the door if the worst comes to the worst, well . . . up he pipes again. Funny excited sort of voice he had. "Lily," he shouts. "That's what I'm going to call you—Lily—because you've got a lovely white bottom!" I'm telling you no lies, those were his very words. I could have died with shame. "Are you aware," I said, "that this is a church and that *Some*one (I said it just like that—*Some*-one) is listening to what you're saying?" "Of course she is," he shouts, making out he hasn't understood what I meant, "and she's got a lovely white bottom and I'm going to FERtilize her!" Well, I saw him start to . . .'

'Just a minute,' said Policewoman Bellweather, her note-taking defeated by the increased pace of the narrative. 'He said he was going to what?'

'FER-tilize me. That's how he said it, oh, really horribly.' She thrust forward her ordinary demure-looking chin to aid the impression. 'FU-U-UR-tilize!'

The policewoman clicked her tongue. 'Right, go on, Mrs Pasquith.'

'Well, I was telling you that I saw him start to move. That was enough for me. Right, I thought, this is where I make myself scarce. And I just ran for that vestry door. Oh dear, I can laugh about it now, but I was really frightened. I mean, when somebody says things like that in a church and then starts coming for you, well. . . . So through that door I went double quick and slam! I'd got it locked. And only just in time, I should say.'

'He chased you?'

'He kept banging on the door and shouting, "Look—no hands!" The filthy beast.'

'So then you telephoned for help, did you, Mrs Pasquith?'

'Well, no, I didn't, actually. I thought I wouldn't give him that satisfaction—you know, to think that he'd scared me into calling for help. I *was* scared, oh yes, but after all I knew I was safe where I was. You see? I thought, *you* won't want to hang about there much longer and risk getting caught. *You*'ll get tired of it before I do, I thought. And so he did. I heard him walk away up the aisle and out the back, and soon afterwards the vicar came in and everything was all right. But I thought I ought to report him because you never know what someone like that might do next. Well . . .'

Policewoman Bellweather frowned. 'Don't you think it would have been wiser to telephone straight away, Mrs Pasquith? It's rather late for us to do anything about the man now.'

'Yes, but you see I didn't really like to. I didn't know what people might think. I mean, he'd said all those horrible things and I couldn't be sure that he wouldn't tell lies if somebody came and caught him. Lies about me, I mean. Well, they do, don't they? And I'm on the flower committee and everything, you see.'

The policewoman did not see. 'But if he *had* told lies, it's most unlikely that they would have been believed surely?'

Mrs Pasquith puckered her flower committee lips in a smile of forgiveness for Miss Bellweather's naïveté.

'When you were making for the vestry door . . .'

'Yes, love?'

'Did you get a better view of what the man looked like? He must have been nearer by then.'

'Well, he was, of course, but I didn't stop to stare, I can tell you. I just sort of caught a glimpse of him out of the corner of my eye, if you see what I mean.'

'You can't give me a description, then? Not even a rough impression?'

Mrs Pasquith shook her head regretfully, but continued to give the matter thought.

'He certainly wasn't a young man, that's all I can tell you.'

'How did he speak?'

'Oh, very impudent, very bold. Well, I told you . . .'

'No, I mean was he an educated sort of man?'

'You might call him that, yes. Well, "pollinate"—I mean that's not a word that somebody ignorant would think of using, is it?'

'I suppose not,' said the policewoman.

There did not seem to be any other question she might usefully ask. The interview had been a waste of time. It had not produced a single clue to the man's identity. So far as she could see, he hadn't even committed a crime. Threatening words and behaviour? Possibly. Conduct likely to lead to a breach of the peace? Well, at a pinch . . .

'There is just one thing,' Mrs Pasquith said suddenly.

'Yes?'

'I told you I saw the man out of the corner of my eye, well, that's right, he was just a sort of shape coming nearer, but there was something about him that I must have noticed because I thought about it later and wondered if I couldn't have been mistaken. You see, he seemed to be coming towards me, well, sideways on, as if he didn't have proper control over his legs.'

The policewoman took conscientious note.

'I suppose,' Mrs Pasquith concluded regretfully, as if admitting the unlikelihood of her own attractions having sparked off the drama, 'that he must have been drinking.'

This explanation did not commend itself to Inspector Purbright. He sat regarding Policewoman Bellweather's typed report with considerable gloom. A mere drunk might have got away with such behaviour once, or even twice, but it was inconceivable that his luck would have held for three forays against the modesty of Flaxborough womankind. Whoever was responsible had reserves of cunning and energy that were not provided by alcohol.

The most depressing aspect of the business was the probability that the man would continue his exploits until gossip about them induced a public scare out of all proportion to the harm of which he was actually capable.

And yet, who could say what that was? The experience of the Sweeting girl had been a good deal more serious than a brush with a randy old eccentric. And a weaker, less determined woman than Brangwyn Butters could have suffered badly in the isolation of Gorry Wood.

No, it was natural enough for people to get frightened while this sort of thing was going on in the town. It was also reasonable—and proper—for them to demand what their police force was doing about it.

The trouble was, as Purbright well knew from past experience of Flaxborough's endemic sexual impetuosity, that the offender invariably was unpredictable as well as wily. He also seemed to have a complaisant wife, acquaintances who had the greatest difficulty in recognizing him at a distance of more than three feet, and a genius for picking victims with delayed reactions and bad memories.

The inspector's mood was not lightened when his telephone rang and he heard the eagerly inquisitive voice of young Henry Popplewell.

'Now then, chiefy, what's all this about the Flaxborough Crab?'

Henry, the son of Mrs Popplewell, Justice of the Peace, was the *Flaxborough Citizen*'s most recently acquired and already regretted junior reporter.

'Crab?' echoed Purbright, in genuine bewilderment.

'That's right. The whole town's talking about him. You know—all this peeping through curtains and chasing women. We've got no end of stories. I'm just tying them up.'

Henry delivered this final information with the pride of some embryo Northcliffe packed umbilically with newspaper jargon.

'I think,' Purbright said, 'that you'd better come along and see me, Mr Popplewell.'

'Will do,' chimed Henry.

Purbright replaced the receiver. He looked pained. He was very much afraid that Henry's 'Will do' was but a foretaste of even heartier abbreviations to come. He waited, nerves tingling, for the door to open and admit Mr Popplewell and his 'Long time no see!'

At last there was a knock and Henry's head appeared.

'Chow!'

The inspector winced.

Henry came in. Purbright pointed invitingly to a chair. Instead of sitting, Henry twirled the chair round behind him and leaned against its back in the manner of a sportsman resting on his shooting stick. He gazed jauntily round the shabby little office.

'And how's tricks?' he asked.

It's coming, thought Purbright, *it MUST be coming.*

Henry stared with open curiosity towards the papers on the inspector's desk. He scratched under his left armpit, yawned, glanced out of the window, then fished a cigarette from the breast pocket of his jacket and lit it, frowning. He expelled smoke as if trying to blow out a candle from ten feet. This seemed to do him a lot of good. He smiled.

'Well, well—long time no see!'

Purbright swallowed and visibly relaxed.

'Mr. Popplewell, you mentioned on the telephone someone or something called the Flaxborough Crab.'

'Right?'

'Who calls him that?'

'Everybody. Either that, or the Flaxborough Strangler.'

The inspector raised his brows.

'I don't recall any reports of stranglings, Mr Popplewell.'

'Ah, you've not heard from that woman in Windsor Close, then? Half a tick . . .' Henry consulted the back of an empty cigarette packet. 'Mrs Cowper, husband on the buses. No joy?

'She's not complained to us.'

'That figures,' said Henry cheerfully. Purbright had no idea what he meant.

'Or Mavis what's-her-name, the waitress at the Roebuck?'

'Another strangling?'

'Do me a favor! No—knicker-snatching, that one.'

Purbright tried to resist the growing sense of confusion that was imparted by the substance and, more particularly, the manner of Henry's conversation. He lit himself a cigarette, examined it carefully, and began:

'I gather that what you are . . .'

'Look,' Henry interrupted, 'can you give me the dope on this peeping angle?'

'Peeping?'

'Natch. All over the place. Women daren't go to bed.'

'Somebody looks through their windows?'

'That's the drill. No one's slept for a fortnight down Edward Crescent or Abdication Avenue. Hey, but you know all this! You have to know. Come on—impart!'

Henry had unpropped himself and was now pacing restlessly up and down, immediately in front of Purbright's desk.

'I'm very much afraid that there is nothing that I *can* impart. It is you who seem to have all the information. There *have* been two assaults recently. The sergeant downstairs will give you the details of those. But as far as the other things are concerned, it seems that you have a—what should I say?—a scoop. Congratulations.'

Henry stopped pacing and eyed Purbright speculatively. Then he nodded.

'Fair enough. Sergeant downstairs? Will do.'

He made for the door.

'Oh, by the way, Mr Popplewell . . .'

Henry turned.

'This soubriquet you say everybody is using. The Flaxborough Crab. I don't quite get the significance.'

For answer, Henry took three or four lurching steps sideways, as if the floor had suddenly become the deck of a ship in heavy seas.

'Runs away like that. So they say.'

'Oh, I see. Thank you very much.'

'Don't mensh.' Henry opened the door and gave a sprightly salute of farewell. 'Chow!'

'Good morning,' said Purbright.

CHAPTER FOUR

Mr Harcourt Chubb, the Chief Constable, listened courteously to his inspector's summary of the activities to date of the Flaxborough Crab.

He had adopted his inevitable audience-giving stance of leaning elegantly against the corner of the fireplace in his office while Purbright sat (at Mr. Chubb's insistence) on a rather low chair six feet away.

Purbright outlined the experiences of Miss Butters and Brenda Sweeting; then added the gleanings of the *Flaxborough Citizen* from the troubled fields of Edward Crescent, Windsor Close and Abdication Avenue.

'I've sent two men over to make inquiries in the area, sir. They have a few addresses. Mr Lintz, the editor of the *Citizen,* was kind enough to let me have a proof of the story that they're running on Friday.'

The Chief Constable pursed his lips. 'Mind you, Mr Purbright, I should be inclined to treat that sort of thing with great reserve. Newspapers, you know . . .' He shook his head sadly.

Purbright was well aware of Mr Chubb's distrust of the Press. Only two weeks previously, in its report of the annual Flaxborough Kennel Club Show, the *Citizen* had emasculated in print his prize-winning Yorkshire Terrier, "Six-shot Rufus of Swaledale", by contriving to substitute its name for that of the Bitch with the Most Appealing Eyes.

'It does seem rather a pity,' Mr Chubb said, 'that we have to get this sort of information at second hand, so to speak. I should have thought that it fell into the category of gossip.'

'We must not despise gossip if it proves useful, sir.'

'No, but don't you think that this fellow might get tired of roaming around and making a nuisance of himself if he isn't encouraged by a lot of fuss? I'll have a word with Lintz, if you like. He owes me a favour.'

Purbright shook his head. 'An editor would want a much better reason than that for suppressing a news item, if you don't mind my saying so. I'm afraid he would tell you that facts are not private property, sir. And he would be right.'

The Chief Constable made a non-committal murmur and looked gravely wise.

'In any case,' Purbright went on, 'I think it will be just as well if the public is put on its guard. This man may have given some pretty futile performances up to now, but I think he's dangerous—potentially dangerous, at any rate. And if we can't warn people, I'm sure you wouldn't want to prevent the newspapers from doing so, sir.'

'Well, not if danger really exists, naturally.'

'I believe it does. That is why I expect you would like me to put as many men as possible on night patrol for a while.'

'I'm sure I can leave you to do what you consider best, Mr Purbright.'

'Thank you, sir.'

The inspector closed the folder he had been holding on his knee and stood up. He was a head taller than the Chief Constable.

Returning to his own office, he discussed with Sergeant Love the deployment of those nocturnal unfortunates whom Love was quick to dub his "Crab-catchers". They agreed that there would be no point in dissipating such meagre resources by trying to cover places like Gorry Wood. Better to give what eye they could to the housing estates within the town boundaries, with special concern for whatever had been troubling the insomniac housewives of Abdication Avenue and its vicinity.

That night, two detectives and five constables gathered in the canteen to be briefed by the inspector.

The detectives looked their usual nondescript selves. The men from the uniformed branch, however, had responded to the instruction to appear in plain, dark clothes by donning their best Sunday suits. They made Purbright think of a bunch of mourners, fortifying themselves with mugs of cocoa before the journey to the cemetery.

After he had assigned them their areas of operation, the inspector told the men what little was known of the characteristics of the quarry. Related badly, it sounded almost useless, and he noticed that several of his troop looked even more like mourners than they had before.

'Couldn't we take some decoys with us, sir?'

This suggestion came from Constable Wilkinson, who rose and stood to attention while making it.

In the ensuing murmur of jocular approval could be distinguished such remarks as 'Comforts for the troops' and 'Where's Sadie Bellweather?'

'I think you'd better see what you can do on your own at this stage, gentlemen,' Purbright said. 'I'm sorry you've so little to work on, but specific information is nearly always lacking in cases of this kind. Victims of sexual assault seldom make good witnesses, as you yourselves will doubtless have found . . .'

He paused, aware of a certain unfortunate ambiguity in his words, and added:

'But this time at least there seems to be general agreement on one feature—the very peculiar manner of running that your man adopts when challenged. I'm sure you will have no difficulty in recognizing it.

'There is just one hazard of which perhaps I ought to remind you before you leave. This man has been reported as varying his more violent activities with spells of window-watching in the areas you have been given to patrol. Now then, it is right and proper that you should watch for the watcher. That is part of your job. But you will, I am sure, be aware of the unfortunate impression that would be created—not least in the minds of vigilant husbands—if your solicitude were to be observed in turn.'

'What he means,' whispered Detective Pook to the stolid constable at his side, "is that you're to keep your eyes off the cheesecake in the bathrooms, mate.'

The seven policemen took their final swigs of cocoa, nodded respectful farewells to the inspector, and filed out into the night. Their duty was to end at two o'clock in the morning, which Purbright and Love had decided between them to be a reasonable upper limit to the libidinous potentialities of even the Crab.

For the next four hours, each officer was to stroll as quietly as he was able up and down the streets of his allotted area, linger here and there in whatever concealed vantage points offered, traverse back lanes, peer into gardens and yards, avoid encounters, resist the lure of carelessly curtained windows, and stave off sleep.

It was not the most congenial assignment he could have wished.

Nor, in any instance, did it achieve its object.

The night's only excitement fell to the lot of Constable Burke.

He had been given surveillance over a group of five interconnecting streets that formed the southern half of the Burton Lane council estate. The area was popularly, if now unjustly, known as "Bottle Hill". This name had been bestowed in days when the place was garrisoned by families of quite remarkably bibulous and quarrelsome tendencies, but no more than three or four of these households had survived the twin ravages of feud and eviction order, and a comparatively conformist type of tenant was now in the majority.

Constable Burke was aware, nevertheless, that the Cutlocks, the O'Shaunessys and the Trings still maintained some of the traditions of a more colourful era. He was not surprised, on passing the home of Grandma Tring and her brood, to hear shrieks suggestive of multiple disembowellings. Nor, when he drew near the scarred homestead known in probation circles as "Cutlock Castle", was he unduly alarmed by the sight of two women trying to pull a third into a bonfire that blazed amidst the weeds of the front garden. It was a little after midnight. The constable strolled on. The prevention of cremations was not in his brief.

What did surprise him very much was the appearance of the O'Shaunessy residence, two hundred yards farther on. With the exception of a single illuminated window on the upper floor, it was in darkness.

Constable Burke halted and ruminated.

He had never before seen the house at any hour of the night otherwise than lit up like a gin palace. This, one supposed, was to facilitate the drift from floor to floor and room to room of the almost perpetual parties and fights that constituted O'Shaunessy hospitality.

Yet tonight the entire galaxy had been snuffed, but for that one lamp upstairs. More strangely still, the place was silent.

For a moment, Constable Burke felt like the first visitor to Glencoe after the departure of the Campbells. Massacre—or perhaps plague—seemed the only possible explanation of the peace that now cloaked the neighbourhood.

Then he glimpsed movement in the one lighted room. There was still life in the house, apparently. He crossed the road and moved slowly towards it.

He was extremely puzzled. Were it not for the survival of that bedroom lamp, the reasonable inference would have been that the family had been obliged to fall back on its reserves by robbing the electricity meter. But the power clearly was still on. In any case, the O'Shaunessys were great improvisers: they would have set light to the staircase sooner than sit drinking in the dark.

Constable Burke was by now just outside the house, close by the front gate. And, perhaps because he was so puzzled, he committed the very error against which the inspector had carefully given warning.

He stared up at the lighted window.

What he saw would have immobilized much less susceptible men.

Just beyond the undraped glass, yet as splendidly indifferent as if it had been solid brick, a young woman was hurriedly removing her clothes.

The constable did not call out. He did not blow his whistle. He made no preparations to note down a name and address with a view to proceedings being taken. He did not even try and think of what Section of what

Act was being contravened. He simply froze into grateful contemplation.

Time, for him, ceased to exist, save perhaps as a season between jumper and skirt, an interval of hair-rumpling, a span from suspender to suspender. Minutes or years could have been going by, for all he could tell. Certainly the girl was in no haste; a less enraptured observer might have suspected that she had in mind a limit to her performance, that she was following some sort of schedule.

No such misgivings clouded the trance of Constable Burke. He continued to stand motionless, deaf, blind to all but the occupant of the shining rectangle in the black sky.

Her remaining garments were now at the count of two. Which next? Oh, delicious speculation. She was facing into the room. Her hand was behind her. It strayed to a point in the middle of her back. No, down now. It lingered at her waist. Ah . . .

'Right! NOW!'

The sound was like that of an exploding boiler.

Immediately in front of Constable Burke there rose up what seemed to his confused senses to be a great column of black smoke shot with scarlet flame.

'I've got him, lads!' boomed the smoke. It swooped and engulfed him with a smell of fish and whiskey. Other shapes crowded in from each side. He was on the ground, flat on his back. Objects of great weight and excruciating hardness bore down his arms and legs, apparently with the purpose of embedding them permanently in the pavement. On to his stomach descended a monument.

The voice again roared out in command. This time, it was directed upward.

'Right y'are, Bernadine—ye'd best be gettin' yerself daicent now and downstairs wid ye!'

The girl in the bedroom snatched one of her discarded garments from the floor, shielded herself behind it and drew the curtains. In other rooms of the house lights sprang on.

They enabled Constable Burke to identify the great red face of the man who sat on his stomach and gazed in ferocious triumph from one to another of the rest of the ambuscados. He was Joseph O'Shaunessy, *père*—Old Dogfish himself—and those who knelt on Burke's limbs were a muster of such sons and sons-in-law as happened currently to be out of prison.

The constable used what breath remained in him to acquaint the O'Shaunessies of his profession and of the heinous nature of the assault they had just committed.

The old man found his recital immensely amusing. He, he responded, was the Pope—as his sons would confirm. The sons did so.

There followed from their father a brief but zestful account of what was proposed to be done with the man who had lurked, night after night, to spy (God forgive him) upon the modesty of good Catholic girls. At tidetime, in two hours, he would be taken aboard the family shrimping boat as far as Cat's Head Middle, or maybe Yorking Passage, and then unladen to peep at mermaids.

'And now,' called the old man, clambering at last from the policeman's midriff, 'let's be havin' 'im inside so's yer mother can stitch some nice big stones into his pockets.'

In possession once more of the gift of speech, Constable Burke declared again who and what he was. This time, there was more light and his face was no longer overshadowed by the anatomy of Old Dogfish. One of the sons clutched his fathers' arm.

'Holy Mother o' God! He's tellin' the truth, Da. It's a rozzer, all right, and from the station house itself!'

Several of the others relinquished their hold on Burke and peered at him anxiously. One turned to his father and nodded. He looked disappointed, like a sportsman on learning his bird to be out of season.

'Jaisus!' muttered the old man. He cuffed those of his retinue that were within reach, then whipped from beneath his jersey a handkerchief the size and colour of a ketch sail and with it began brushing down the constable's jacket and trousers.

'No harm done, sor! No harm at all. We can all make a little mistake sometimes, now can't we, sor?'

He gave one of his sons an affectionate kick. 'And what are yous all standin' there for, ye great gawps? Get inside wid ye and tell yer mother to have a nice cup o' tay ready for the gentleman.'

And so amends were made—not only with draughts of tea like concentrated wood preservative, but with lacings of "the hard stuff" and genial pledges to the Boys in Blue, and smiles and dimplings from a now dressed and demure Bernadine and, as a finale, a newspaper-enwrapped lobster with compliments of the guest's Good Lady.

In so jolly an atmosphere, it was hardly to be expected that anybody would notice the rising of a figure from concealment near the front gate and its rapid yet curiously clumsy departure into the darkness.

CHAPTER FIVE

At ten o'clock the next morning, while Inspector Purbright was hearing details of the first and fruitless watch for the Flaxborough Crab, a bus drew up outside the Trent Street Darby and Joan Club. Thirty-five of the members were waiting to be taken on their annual outing.

This year's venue was to be the old reservoir at Gosby Vale, a half-hour's drive distant. There would be a picnic lunch, games, and a competition based on the naming of wild flowers. Lemonade a-plenty (in the terminology of the organizers) was to be available and an optimistic rumour had persisted in the club for some weeks that a crate of light ale for the gentlemen had been donated by the Flaxborough Brewery Company.

This, indeed, was true, but the organizers had thought it politic to hide the crate in the back of the luggage compartment of the bus as a reserve benefaction. It would be withheld if circumstances suggested that undue frivolity might result.

At the moment, no such eventuality seemed likely or even possible. There was an air of sober resignation about the party of old men and women assembled in one corner of the club concert room. Despite the warmth of the day, they were in thick outdoor clothing. All wore hats. Some, with suitcases or parcels at their feet, looked like emigrants awaiting passage to Hudson Bay.

The chief organizer of the treat bustled into the room, rubbing his hands and saying 'Fine! Fine!' over and over again. He hosed the Darbys and Joans down with his smile and inflicted a vigorous handshake upon as many as lacked the presence of mind to feign earnest search for something on the floor.

He was Steven Winge, shipping broker, lay preacher, alderman of Flaxborough Town Council, masonic brother, and ever-jocular claimant to being "sixty-eight years young".

Hard behind Alderman Winge came his lieutenant, Miss Bertha Pollock.

She was a short, stout woman, compactly encased in a black silk dress. She had little pointed legs and one felt that if whipped she would spin rather nicely. Her hat, which she wore everywhere, was tight as a lid and the colour of lips in heart failure.

Miss Pollock, too, was armed with a smile.

'Brought your knitting, dear? That's nice.' She patted, in the manner of a dog-lover, the grey head of old Mrs Crunkinghorn.

These preliminary greetings by Alderman Winge and Miss Pollock signalled the descent of further helpers into the flock of supine treatees. Mostly female, plump, voluble and well-heeled, but inclusive of a couple of lean men with forgiving, other-worldly faces, and hands that seemed always to be distributing invisible hymn books, these people moved among the Darbys and the Joans, shepherding, cajoling, taking away chairs, smiling the obstinate into submission, breaking with cheerfulness the groups of passive resisters, helpfully confiscating luggage—until the last stragglers had been manoeuvred from the room and marshalled into the waiting coach.

The treat had begun.

Alderman Winge and Miss Pollock occupied a double seat at the front of the coach, immediately behind the driver. They took turns throughout the journey to swivel round and review the passengers with 'Everybody all right? Goo-oo-ood!' These commending surveys seemed also to have the object of a quick check on numbers, as though the possibility of escapes had not been ruled out.

The Darbys and Joans stared impassively through the windows at streets in which most of them had spent their entire lives. Occasionally, one or another of the women would raise her fingers and wave shyly at an old acquaintance glimpsed among the shoppers. The men did not do this. Only when buildings gave way to fields and the sole spectators of the coach's passing were mournful-eyed cows, did they relax their posture of dignified suffering and peer with interest at the countryside.

'Isn't that lovely?' loudly inquired Miss Pollock of the company at large. For some reason or other, she had moved to a vacant seat on the other side of the gangway. A few of the women obediently murmured assent. Old Mrs Crunkinghorn got out her handkerchief in preparation for a bout of her congestion.

Through Pennick village the coach rolled, and on towards Hambourne. Heat shimmered in patches on the straight stretch of road ahead like sheets of water that evaporated before one reached them. Inside the coach, speculation concerning the gift of the brewery was renewed. Most were inclined to accept its nonappearance as proof of the folly of believing in miracles, but this did not prevent other theories being offered. The wildest, and therefore the most attractive, attributed the party's loss to the secret thirst of Alderman Winge himself.

Unaware of this calumny, the alderman swung round in his seat, beamed at his detractors, and called: 'Now then, ladies and gentlemen, what about a sing-song?'

"What about our beer?' retorted somebody at the back.

The alderman's smile remained undimmed.

'Daisy, Daisy—how about that one, eh? Right, then. *Dai-ai-see, Dai-ai-see . . .*' He made measured, encouraging motions with his raised arm. 'That's fine—*Give me your a-answer, do-oo . . .*'

'I'm half cra-a-zy, all for the love of you-oo . . .' Thus, in a curdling contralto that somehow was as unlikely as the sentiment it expressed, did Miss Pollock give loyal support. No one else did.

'Ah, well,' said Alderman Winge, 'perhaps it's a little early for us all to be in voice, eh? Never mind. What about a round or two of I Spy? Now wait a moment. . . . I spy with my little eye . . . something beginning with . . .' He glanced inquisitively around the coach.

'With B for beer,' came again the voice of the hidden malcontent.

'No, no . . . wait a minute. . . . Something that begins with C,' announced the alderman, serenely.

The passengers cast dubious looks at where they thought Alderman Winge had detected his object. They saw nothing significant. Only old Mrs Crunkinghorn made any response.

'Cow?' she suggested, staring straight at Miss Pollock.

Ten minutes later, the coach passed through North

Gosby and descended into the greenery of Gosby Vale.

The old reservoir was at the end of a narrow lane, about half a mile from the main road. It was a natural lake, bordered on three sides by woods. The fourth side was a grass-covered embankment, steeply shelved to the water but declining much more gradually to the meadowland it protected and with which it now seemed merged.

It was in this meadow that the party was intended to receive the benefits of sunshine, fresh air and rural peace.

The coach drew up on a patch of concrete where once a pumping station had stood. Alderman Winge, Miss Pollock and the helpers climbed out to be ready with support for the less agile members of the party.

Slowly, the coach emptied. A case of food and a crate of lemonade were disinterred and carried to a shady spot at the edge of the meadow. The ale was left where it was.

Alderman Winge ran a benevolent eye over the assembly, most of whom seemed at a loss to know what they were expected to enjoy first. He set example by thrusting his head back and ecstatically sucking in a chestful of air, which, after four or five seconds, he discharged as if it had been an entire chapter of Ecclesiastes.

Miss Pollock took a more modest helping. She pronounced it to be 'like wine!' ('How would *she* know?' muttered old Mrs Crunkinghorn to a neighbour.)

A few experimental sniffs having failed to convince anybody that breathing alone was going to make the day memorable, the Darbys and Joans began to wander off in small groups.

'That's right!' Miss Pollock called after them. 'Go

and pick some nice flowers, all of you. We'll have the naming competition straight after lunch.'

Some flowers were, in fact, picked—mainly by those who had conceived the notion that participation in the meal would be made conditional upon fulfilment of Miss Pollock's command.

The others occupied themselves in a variety of ways. Some sought refuge in the nearby woods for a quiet smoke. Most of the women got as far as they could from the platoon of helpers milling round the picnic basket and sat in the long grass to knit and gossip. The anglers in the party instinctively drew together to climb the bank and gaze for two silent hours into the deep, weed-streaked water of the reservoir. One man, who still remembered a country upbringing, spent the morning stalking a pheasant which he managed eventually to grab, execute, and stow away under his coat.

All were rallied shortly after the mid-day by the admonitory hoots of Miss Pollock. Food, or, as Alderman Winge preferred to express it, "our little feast", was ready.

The sun was high now and by the time the meal was over a pleasant apathy had settled upon almost all the company. One or two removed their overcoats. Sleep seemed a very good idea.

But not to Miss Pollock.

Clapping her hands to jerk the somnolent back to the business of being made happy, she announced that the flower naming competition would be held forthwith.

'Some of you' (there was the tiniest reproving emphasis on the "some") 'have collected lots of absolutely lovely flowers, and we must see now—mustn't we?—how many of them you can name. Now then, I'll hold up each of these nice little flowers in turn, and I want you to call out its name. Mr. Winge is going to keep the score—aren't you, Mr. Winge?—so that we shall know who gets the most right. Ready, everybody? Now here's an easy one for a start.'

She held aloft a dandelion.

'That's naught but a poor little piss-a-bed,' declared old Mrs Crunkinghorn promptly and with disdain.

Miss Pollock looked taken aback. 'Well, actually, I would have thought . . .'

'That's what that is,' Mrs Crunkinghorn affirmed. 'A poor little piss-a . . .'

'Yes, the old country name, I expect. Ah, now what's this next one, I wonder?'

In her hand was a straggle of stalk from which hung several diminutive white bells.

'Tickle-titty,' said Mrs Crunkinghorn, without hesitation. 'That's what that is, my old duck.'

Hastily, Miss Pollock put it down and selected what she was sure was a perfectly innocent wood anemone.

Again, Mrs Crunkinghorn's was the sole responding voice.

'Poke-me-Gently. Very good for green-sickness, my mother always reckoned.'

On to the discard pile went the specimen of Poke-me-Gently. Raising another flower—a lank, brownish-yellow affair—Miss Pollock deliberately avoided the leading contestant's eye and looked appealingly to the further part of her audience.

'Now, what about some of you other ladies? Wouldn't you like to have a try?'

'Old Man's Vomit,' snapped the omniscient Mrs Crunkinghorn. 'You don't want to hold that too near your dress, me dear.'

Miss Pollock looked at Alderman Winge, inwardly urging him to declare the competition won and over, but all he did was rub his hands and say to Mrs Crunkinghorn: 'My, my! I can see that you have been a botanist in your time, dear lady!'

'I've had me ups and downs,' confirmed Mrs. Crunkinghorn, with a leer.

By now thoroughly apprehensive, Miss Pollock displayed flower number five.

'Haahrr . . . Purple Lechery!' Mrs Crunkinghorn showed that when it came to hand rubbing she was the equal of any alderman.

'Now, dear,' Miss Pollock said to her, 'I think you have had a very fair innings, don't you? You really must be a good sport and let the others have a chance. It won't be a proper competition if only one lady takes part, will it?'

Having made another selection, Miss Pollock held it up in such a way that her hand shielded it from Mrs Crunkinghorn's view. The flower was tubular and of an unsavoury pink, mottled with green: it looked like a tiny bloodshot cucumber.

Nearly a minute went by.

'Come along,' said Miss Pollock. 'Isn't anyone going to have a guess?'

A stolid silence.

Miss Pollock's arm grew tired. She transferred the flower to her other hand. For one instant, it was in unrestricted view.

A caw of gleeful recognition, and Mrs Crunkinghorn scored yet again.

'Squire Stinkfinger!' she cried, then hugged herself in a transport of chucklesome reminiscence.

'I-I don't think th-that . . .' stammered Miss Pollock, her face much the same colour as the flower she had just tossed disgustedly to the ground. 'Perhaps now we, we should . . .' Without thinking, she seized another piece of flora and began twisting it in her fingers. 'Perhaps . . .'

'Maids in a Sweat!' Mrs Crunkinghorn's final triumphant identification rang out like the game-stopping call of a Bingo victor.

She wagged a bony finger at Miss Pollock.

'Never you put none o' *that* under your pillow, me old duck! Goorrh! Not unless you want some o' what you ain't never 'ad!'

To the rescue at last came Alderman Winge. He raised his arms in an all-embracing gesture and announced that what they needed more than anything else at that moment was a jolly good game to settle their meal. Hide-and-Seek, no less. The ladies would hide (as they always did, ha-ha) and the gentlemen would seek. He looked at his watch.

'Five minutes' start for the fair sex, eh? Right, off you go, ladies!'

He beckoned Miss Pollock and lowered his voice.

'Some of the dear old souls are just a little slow to get into the swing of things. I think it's rather up to us to give them a lead. If you, dear lady, would be good enough to go over into that little thicket yonder, I shall wait here a few minutes and then pretend to look for you. Would you do that? Capital!'

Miss Pollock nodded and set off. Alderman Winge ostentatiously covered his eyes with his hands and bayed encouragement to the slowly dispersing and reluctant Joans. Four remained where they were on the ground. They appeared to be asleep.

After five minutes, Mr Winge uncovered his eyes and signalled the old men to depart in pursuit. Grumpily they lumbered away towards the trees. Mr. Winge, affecting uncertainty, began a zig-zag course that would take him to Miss Pollock's hiding place.

The abandoned sleepers buzzed and snorted contentedly in the sun. One was Mrs Crunkinghorn. As soon as she judged it safe to abandon her strategem, she sat up, made herself comfortable, and got on with her knitting.

The helpers were in the coach, enjoying cups of tea that they had brewed privately on a paraffin stove. With them was the driver. No one else was in sight, although an occasional distant squeal of surprise indicated where some at least of the hiders and seekers were entering belatedly into the spirit of the game. Of the two organizers, there was no sign.

Mrs Crunkinghorn's knitting needles clattered on. She felt pleased with herself, with the sunshine she had been allowed at last to enjoy in peace, and with the bees that hummed in the clover flowers about her. Her thoughts strayed into other fields in other, far-off times when she was a girl at Moldham Marsh. Moldham. . . . *Like lookin' fer maiden' eads at Moldham*—that's what they used to say when anything was rare or difficult. Aye, and no wonder. . . . She rocked over her knitting and gave a ghostly little cackle in tribute to lads who were dodderers now, or dust. . . .

Suddenly, the old woman perked up her head. Who, she asked herself, was that—scrawking like a guinea-hen? She sat straight and shaded her eyes with one hand while she peered across the meadow in the direction of the scream.

A figure emerged from a copse at the far corner of the meadow. It was that of a small, dumpy woman. She pelted like mad out of the trees, arms pumping, knees high. Mrs Crunkinghorn stared admiringly.

Seconds later, there broke from the same cover a taller, lankier runner—a man. His limbs flailed loosely and he seemed to have trouble in keeping his balance, but he was covering the ground at no less a rate than his quarry. In one hand he clutched a strip of what looked like dark cloth that fluttered behind him in the slipstream.

The woman raced across the grass for twenty or thirty yards, the man gaining noticeably. He reached out, almost touched her; but then she veered and began to run at a tangent up the slope of the reservoir. By the time she reached the top, the distance between them had increased by a couple of yards.

Still no one else had appeared to witness the chase. Mrs Crunkinghorn felt a sense of privilege.

The figures now were silhouetted against the sky, and the watcher had a clear picture of the drama's startlingly odd end.

The man had no sooner levelled into pursuit along the top of the embankment than his body seemed to turn on its own axis, quite independently of the legs. Considerably inconvenienced by this lack of co-ordination, the legs, though still pounding along, began first to knock against each other and then to swing out at increasingly wild angles.

It seemed to Mrs Crunkinghorn that the man was actually running sideways.

But soon he was not running at all. The legs having become hopelessly entangled with each other, he stumbled and cart-wheeled on to his head, then toppled, quite slowly, over the farther edge of the embankment.

Mrs Crunkinghorn was too far off to hear the splash.

CHAPTER SIX

Miss Pollock heard it, though. She stopped running and turned. What she saw made her scream, but not quite as loudly as she had screamed before. She remained where she was just long enough to get wind for another sprint, then she set off down the bank towards the coach, frantically waving one arm.

Three minutes later, a group of intrigued but helpless people stood on the brink of the reservoir, staring down at the submerged features of Alderman Steven Winge.

The body was only about a foot below the surface. It undulated very, very slowly, as if lazily flexing and relaxing in the cool luxury of effortless suspension. Mr Winge looked remote, certainly, but not dead. His eyes were wide open and he was smiling as usual. One hand still grasped its trophy of torn cloth, a black pennant drifting down to mingle with fronds of weed.

One of the helpers glanced surreptitiously at the rent in Miss Pollock's dress.

The coach driver was the first to speak.

'I'll get off to a phone. You'd better stay where you are.'

He went down the banking at a half run. At the bottom, he shouted over his shoulder:

'And don't try and do anything—you'll only fall in yourselves.'

The pensioners were beginning to straggle back in twos and threes, attracted by the sounds of crisis. The word spread that something dreadful had happened to Mr Winge. The old men and women toiled up the bank to see for themselves.

The body neither sank nor rose. It did not shift perceptibly in any direction at all. It seemed set for ever in dim, green jelly.

'What 'yer doin' down there, Mr Winge?' quavered potty old Mrs Baxter.

Shocked, the others shushed her. Yet they, too, found it a little hard to think of a man dead who could continue to smile with such patent self-congratulation.

Soon after three o'clock, there sounded faintly through the trees the double candy-trumpet notes of an approaching fire tender. It emerged from the lane, scarlet, strident, splendid; drove at undiminished speed across the meadow, and rocked to a halt at the top of the banking.

Four firemen in unbuttoned tunics and shiny black thigh boots climbed out and unshipped ropes and straps and what looked like enormous fishing hooks. Carrying their gear, they pushed courteously but firmly past the watchers.

A police car drew up below, closely followed by an ambulance.

The firemen's task did not take long. When the retrieved body had been laid to drain for a few minutes and then stretcher-borne to the ambulance, they neatly re-coiled their ropes, smoked a cigarette apiece, and drove back to town.

One of the two policemen, in deference to those

parts of Miss Pollock displayed through the tear in her dress, ushered her to the car.

The other officer went round asking questions. He received the eager undertaking of the sole witness—Mrs Crunkinghorn—to accompany him back to the police station and there describe what had happened.

At ten minutes to four, a procession set off on the return journey to Flaxborough.

It was led by the ambulance. Then came the coach carrying the Darbys and Joans and the helpers and the crate of light ale, unbroached and all but forgotten. In the police car behind, one officer had shifted to the back seat in the company of Miss Pollock so that Mrs Crunkinghorn might enjoy the high spot of her outing—a silent but triumphant homecoming beside the driver.

On reaching town, the three vehicles broke formation and went their separate ways, the ambulance to the mortuary at the General Hospital, the coach to its occupants' club in Trent Street, and the car to police headquarters, where Inspector Purbright and the Coroner's Officer, Sergeant William Malley, were waiting to see what they could make of the stories of its passengers.

In respect for her age, and on the assumption that she would be anxious to get home and rest after the day's excitement, Mrs Crunkinghorn was interviewed first. Meanwhile, Policewoman Bellweather found a raincoat to cover the deficiencies of Miss Pollock's clothing and a mug of tea to restore her spirits.

The inspector soon learned how mistaken had been his expectation of a frail, distressed and inarticulate octagenarian. Mrs Crunkinghorn's description of what she had seen on the sky-line in Gosby Vale had all the colour and fervor of a racing commentary. Purbright was impressed, if a trifle dazed.

He asked her to repeat what she had said about the late alderman's unorthodox manner of pursuit.

'Sideways,' she declared again. 'Sideways wuz 'ow 'e wuz bowlin' along. Until 'is legs' got all raffled up. Then over 'e went, arse over tit! I never seen the like, never. Arse over tit, 'e went! Pwosh!'

'It is very tempting,' Purbright said to Sergeant Malley when the old woman had departed after laboriously scrawling her name at the bottom of the statement typed by Malley, 'to conclude from this that the Flaxborough Crab, so called, is no more.'

Malley stroked one of his chins and wheezed reflectively.

'Aye,' he said. 'It certainly looks like it.'

'He's been a singularly busy man, has our Steve. They tell me he was on fifteen committees.'

The sergeant inflated plump cheeks and shook his head in wonder.

'Sunday school superintendent. Old people's welfare visitor. Magistrate . . .'

'Governor of the Grammar School,' Malley supplied.

'Lifeboat Fund president.'

'Chairman of that television clean-up thing . . .'

For a while, both men sat in awed contemplation of the late alderman's multiplicity of office and honour.

'I wonder,' said Purbright at last, 'what set the old bugger off on this lark all of a sudden. Surely not Miss Pollock?'

Malley shuddered. He sighed and went to the door.

Miss Pollock made her entrance with as much dignity as was possible within the folds of a garment so over-long for her that its hem swept the floor. With her hat still jammed in straight and stern bisection of her forehead, she looked like a helmeted and caped member of a decontamination squad.

At Purbright's invitation, she perched herself grimly on the edge of a chair. Invisible behind the spare yards of raincoat, her little pointed feet dangled three inches from the floor.

The inspector spoke gently.

'This is a very sad and upsetting affair, Miss Pollock, and I'm sorry that you should be put to the trouble of answering questions so soon afterwards. I am sure you understand, though, that the coroner will have to have a clear picture of what happened, and that it will be best to try and put it together straight away.'

'Yes, I see that, of course.' Her voice was firmer, and colder, than Purbright had expected.

'We have heard,' he went on, 'something of the events of this afternoon from the old lady who saw your . . . your predicament from where she was sitting some forty or fifty yards away. She could not tell us, of course, why you appeared to be running away from Mr Winge, nor for what reason he seemed to be chasing you.'

Ignoring the implicit question, Miss Pollock stared at him blankly.

'Perhaps,' said Purbright, 'you could help us with those points.'

Her gaze moved to the window.

'I ran because I was alarmed by Mr Winge's behaviour. It was quite inexplicable.'

Malley, who liked his witnesses' depositions to be chronologically straightforward, put in: 'Before you say anything about that, Miss Pollock, I'd just like to be clear as to where you both were and what you were doing.'

The inspector nodded.

'We were in a small wood—a spinney, I suppose you might call it—in the far corner of the field.'

'Close against the reservoir?'

'Yes. You see, we had set the old folk off on a game of hide-and-seek, and . . .'

'Hide-and-*seek?*' echoed Purbright.

'That is what I said. They like to be occupied, these old people—organized and occupied. But one or two do tend to be laggards, you know, and so we have to give them a lead. That is why Mr Winge suggested that he and I should pretend to be taking part in the game. I went across to the spinney while Mr Winge waited with the old gentlemen. Then he came looking for me—except that he knew where I was, of course.'

'So he joined you in the wood, did he?'

'Yes. We were to wait until all the others were properly on the move and then come back to the coach.'

'You say this had been his suggestion?' the inspector asked.

'Certainly,' declared Miss Pollock, tight-faced.

'You sound as if you had—what shall I say?—misgivings, perhaps?'

'I did.'

'Why?'

'Because Mr Winge had already given me the impression that he was not quite himself. I had been obliged to change seats on the coach soon after we left town.'

Purbright did not ask her to elaborate. Malley put the next question.

'What was the alderman's behaviour in the wood that alarmed you, Miss Pollock?'

'He . . . he made a suggestion.'

'Yes?'

They waited. Miss Pollock let them.

'What was the suggestion?' Purbright prompted. 'It is relevant, you know.'

After further hesitation, she said: 'It was an indecent suggestion. It related to something I was wearing.'

'*Was* wearing?' Malley's big, gentle face was absolutely innocent.

'Was and am!' snapped Miss Pollock.

'Very well,' Purbright said. 'We'll leave it at that. Mr Winge proposed something that offended your sense of decency. How did you react?'

'I told him that he must be mad. This, I may say, I regretted at once because I realized that madness was the only possible explanation and I was afraid that what I had said might provoke him to violence.'

'And did it?'

'Not immediately. He just laughed and made the same suggestion again. I turned and started to walk away. It was then that he attacked me.'

'Can you describe the attack? What he actually did, I mean.'

'I am not altogether certain, but I think he jumped on me from behind. All I remember now is running and feeling something tugging at me. He must have got hold of my dress. It was not until afterwards that I found it was torn.'

'I understand from the policewoman that you didn't suffer any harm physically,' Purbright said.

'Well, no—he didn't hurt me. He didn't get the chance.'

'I am very glad of that, anyway. Now tell me, Miss Pollock, did you at any time while you were running away look back at Mr Winge?'

'Once, yes. It was just before . . . just before the accident.'

'You saw him there behind you—running.'

'Yes.'

'And did you notice anything about the *way* he was running? Was there anything peculiar about it?'

She looked sharply at the inspector, then at Sergeant Malley. 'Should there have been?'

Malley shrugged. Purbright said: 'I was just wondering.'

'I got no more than a sort of flash of him,' said Miss Pollock, guardedly. 'Out of the corner. But it is quite true that he ran in a funny way. I don't quite know how to describe it. He seemed to have half turned round, if you see what I mean, and to be coming sideways on.'

After a short pause, the inspector said: 'And that was the last you saw of him before the accident?'

She nodded.

'Which you heard rather than saw, I presume?'

'I heard a splash, but somehow I didn't connect it with what had been happening up to then. It was only when I looked back and saw that Mr Winge was not there behind me any more, that I realized that he had fallen in.'

'Did you see him in the water?' Malley asked.

'Not at that time. He had disappeared altogether. But I knew what must have happened because the surface was still rocking and swirling about.'

'You ran for help?'

'Naturally.'

Malley turned to the inspector.

'There's nothing the lady could have done herself, sir. The reservoir embankment on the water side is very steep just there—more like a wall.'

'Quite,' said Purbright.

He gave Miss Pollock a reassuring smile.

'You've been extremely helpful. There is only one more question that I should like to ask—and please don't take it as reflecting in any way upon yourself. I simply want to know if there was anything you noticed in Mr Winge's attitude or behaviour before today that suggested his having sexual designs on you or anybody else—on women generally, in fact.'

A geranium flush spread rapidly from neck to hat brim.

'Never! Certainly not! I have worked with Mr Winge for many years and known him up to that quite inexplicable affair today as a public-spirited and very religious gentleman!'

'Thank you, Miss Pollock. We are deeply obliged to you.'

Purbright rose and walked to the door.

The raincoat, surmounted by Miss Pollock's round and indignant little head, glided out.

As the door closed, Malley suddenly flapped his hand in the air.

'Hey, hang on a minute . . . what about her statement?' He wound a sheet of paper into the typewriter.

Purbright said never mind, the deposition could be signed later; he'd have it sent round to her.

Thoughtfully, he resumed his seat beside the big, shabby desk.

'You know, Bill,' he said, 'I don't think she was quite as unprepared for old Steve's crack at her virtue as she pretends.'

Malley began jabbing keys with two plump forefingers. 'Oh, aye?' He watched the keys closely all the time, as if some might otherwise escape their share of punishment.

'I reckon she'd seen signs before. Her reaction to my asking her was a little too righteous to be convincing.'

Malley grunted. He was scraping out a misplaced letter with the tip of what looked like a hunting knife.

'Mind you,' Purbright went on, 'it would be surprising if Winge *had* managed to gallop round like a rutting stag night after night without somebody noticing something. Even Doctor Jekyll couldn't stop Mr Hyde peeping out occasionally at an inconveni . . .'

'They tell me you've got the Crab!'

In the doorway had appeared the cherubic features of Sergeant Love, bright with good news.

'So it would seem,' said Purbright. 'You can let your young lady out again now, Sid.'

Love closed the door carefully behind him.

'My landlady won't half be disappointed,' he said. 'She's been going up as far as the canal end every night this week, in hopes.'

'Have you fixed the inquest yet, Bill?'

'Tomorrow afternoon. Old Amblesby's down in Cornwall, or somewhere, so I've had to call out Thompson. He's not sat as deputy coroner since 1953. He's bloody terrified.'

'I don't know that he need be,' said Purbright, lightly. 'It's a straightforward enough case.'

Malley stopped typing and looked around.

'Didn't I tell you who was doing the P.M., then?'

'No, you didn't, as a matter of fact.'

'Heineman.'

'Oh,' said Purbright. He looked a fraction less carefree.

'And perhaps I didn't mention that Winge's family are getting both his solicitor and his own doctor to attend the inquest.'

'Solicitor. . . .' Purbright frowned. 'That wouldn't be Justin Scorpe, would it?'

'It would.'

'And who's the doctor?'

'Meadow.'

Love looked blandly from the inspector to the coroner's officer.

'What's the idea, then?'

'The family'—Malley leaned back in his chair and champed experimentally on the stem of a squat, black pipe—'are not very pleased.'

He fished a tobacco tin from the distorted breast pocket of his tunic, levered off its lid, and began ramming liquorice-like strands into the pipe bowl.

'I fancy that what they'll be putting Meadow up to say is that the old man was suffering from something or other that caused him to be unaware of what he was doing. You know—very sad, but a sight more respectable than jumping on young women just because he felt like it.'

Love showed by a shrewd pursing of lips that he understood the logic of such strategy. He looked at the inspector.

Purbright murmured to himself: 'Thompson . . . Heineman . . . Meadow . . .'

'They're all doctors, you see,' Malley explained to Love.

'So what?'

'So,' said Malley, with great cheerfulness, 'they all hate one another's guts.'

CHAPTER SEVEN

The ignominious but, most citizens agreed, not undeserved end of the Flaxborough Crab was common knowledge long before the inquest was opened in the little dun-coloured courtroom adjoining the police station.

Alderman Steven Winge had been one of those public figures whose appearance on platforms, at committee tables and in chairs of jurisdiction and debate would seem to be inevitable and of limitless term. No week in the past thirty years had gone by without his having declared something open, or moved a vote of some kind, or given careful consideration to all the facts of a disturbing case.

Except in his role of magistrate, which entailed nothing but determination and sorrow, if Mr Winge's court pronouncements were to be believed, his every duty in a lifetime's service to the Flaxborough community had been prefaced by the assertion: "It gives me great pleasure . . ."

If bliss be a cumulative emotion, one could only assume that the waters of Gosby Reservoir had closed upon a supremely happy man.

But it was now plain to all that there had been another field of activity, private as distinct from public, that had engaged the alderman's energies. It doubtless also had given him great pleasure. Would that day's official inquiry in Fen Street unearth the regrettable details? Flaxborough devoutly hoped so.

The deputy coroner, Dr Thompson, took his seat at two o'clock precisely. He had been looking at his watch all morning and had spent the last half-hour lurking nervously in the corridors of the police station. Public office did not give *him* great pleasure; he cursed the proper holder of this particular one, Mr Albert Amblesby, as an irresponsible, cavorting, brain-softened old absentee. Which was not strictly fair, as the real coroner—admittedly senile, but in general reliably on hand—was at that moment comatose in a Cornish nursing home after falling downstairs during a visit to his married daughter in Truro.

Sergeant Malley, unhurried, efficient, kindly, stood behind Dr Thompson's right shoulder. He held a sheaf of depositions ready to be slipped one by one in their right order before the deputy coroner as the witnesses were called.

Purbright was at the corner of the table farthest from Thompson. Next to him sat Dr Heineman, pathologist at the General Hospital. Also at the table, equidistant from Heineman and the deputy coroner, and carefully refraining from meeting the eye of either, was Dr Meadow.

The non-medical witnesses—Miss Pollock, Mrs Crunkinghorn, a fireman called Hackett, and the alderman's widow, Mrs Olivia Winge—occupied a row of chairs beneath the room's only window.

In a chair on his own, notebook on knee, was Henry Popplewell, of the *Citizen*.

At four minutes past two, a man arrived carrying a briefcase, a pile of books, and a spectacle case that might at a pinch have accommodated a brace of duelling pistols. He glanced mournfully round the court and took a place at the table opposite the deputy coroner by economically combining a deep bow with the motion of sitting down.

'Good afternoon, Mr Scorpe,' said the deputy coroner.

The solicitor gave him a small secondary bow and set about arranging his library. Then he unloaded the contents of the briefcase. Finally, he signified his readiness to allow the inquiry to proceed by donning with a flourish his huge, black-framed spectacles.

Malley leaned towards the deputy coroner's ear.

'Perhaps you'd like to hear the doctors first, sir, so that they can get away.'

Dr Thompson agreed to the concession with prim nervousness. It was the first decision he had been called upon to make that afternoon, the first chance of trying out his voice. He thought it sounded squeaky and resolved to try for more sonority next time.

At a sign from the sergeant, Dr Heineman bounced to his feet and took the oath in a cheery, mittel-European voice. He was a man of brisk and decided manner. His short hair stood up like a brush; it and his high, eloquent eyebrows gave him an air of being the bearer of encouraging tidings. He wore a smartly cut black jacket over a pale pleated shirt. His bow tie was of the jaunty, pre-fabricated kind. It was bright green.

Dr Meadow absorbed these details with blank, slowly ranging eye. Then he slumped carefully in his chair and took a peep under the table. It confirmed his suspicion. The pathologist was wearing spats.

'Doctor, you conducted a post-mortem examination of the body of the deceased at Flaxborough General

Hospital, I understand.' The deputy coroner tried not to look at the green tie.

'Igsectly. Thet I hev done. Yes.' And off went Heineman on a rapid recital of his findings, most of which, if one were to judge by the eagerness of his tone and aspect, were eminently to his taste.

The deceased, he said, was a well-nourished male person aged about sixty. There was some evidence of circulatory deterioration, but no more than was to be expected in a man of his age. All organs were in a comparatively sound condition, and he had been unable to detect by standard pathological techniques any significant degree of physical regression attributable to the age factor.

He *had* been able to eliminate the possibility of intervention in the form of incision, ligature, toxin or concussion.

The deceased had ingested between six and seven ounces of protein and carbohydrate, with traces of mineral compounds, not more than one hour previous to death. No part of the contents of his stomach was inconsistent with normal nutritional processes.

The bone structure of the body appeared to be sound, apart from a healed fracture, many years old, of a bone in the left forearm.

No natural teeth survived in either the lower or the upper jaw.

He had observed a bruise, together with adjacent abrasion, minor in character, in the upper area of the left hip. There were several smaller bruises distributed over both legs. On the left shoulder was an abrasion, while on the right knee . . .

'Correct me if I am wrong, doctor,' broke in the deputy coroner, made daring by boredom, 'but I take it that what you are listing now are the body's superficial injuries—the incidental injuries?'

Heineman pretended to find the interruption incomprehensible. He turned upon Malley a look of sweetly helpful inquiry: it implied that the sergeant was Dr Thompson's keeper and was trained to translate his utterances into rational language.

Thompson frowned. 'You do not suggest, do you, doctor, that the injuries you have been describing were contributory to this man's death? That is all I am asking.'

Heineman looked at the ceiling, then at Inspector Purbright. He gave Purbright a knowing smile, glanced back to his notes, and went on with the report as if no one else had spoken.

He was now happily exploring the complex world of Winge's cranium.

Purbright understood singularly little of this part of the pathologist's evidence, but as he listened and looked to see what others were making of it, two things became clear. Heineman had made some discovery by which he was genuinely intrigued. And Meadow—who up to then had affected absolute indifference—was paying careful attention to what Heineman was saying.

Mr Scorpe, too, seemed gravely interested, but since that particular expression was habitual with him—it had been called his "working face"—Purbright could not be certain that he really found the matter significant.

Dr Thompson offered no further interruption. Only when the pathologist had sat down, beaming his congratulations to the audience on their having enjoyed such a marvellous lecture, did he enquire, with malevolent ingenuousness, whether Dr Heineman was not in a position to suggest a cause of death.

Heineman's eyes popped with amused surprise.

'Cows of dith? But drownink! What ilse?'

'Thank you, doctor. You might have mentioned it earlier.'

The deputy coroner wrote something on the sheet before him. He looked up.

'Would anyone like to ask Dr Heineman any questions? Inspector?'

Purbright shook his head.

'Dr Meadow?'

Meadow declined. Fastidiously.

'Mr Scorpe—you represent the family of the deceased, I understand. . . .'

Scorpe bobbed his great solemn head. '*If* you please.'

'Is there anything you would care to ask the witness?'

Scorpe rose menacingly and re-arranged some of his books, like sandbags before a redoubt. 'A couple of points, doctor, if you wouldn't mind. . . .'

'Pliss!'

Scorpe looked down at the carbon copy of Heineman's report with which the helpful Malley had provided him.

'You say that you found clear indications of a certain neurological condition known as Grosserbayer's Syndrome.'

Heineman nodded. He looked very affable.

'This condition being, in the language of the layman, a disturbance of the brain. . . .'

'Of the cintral neerwus system,' Heineman corrected, one finger raised.

'*If* you please. A disturbance of the central nervous system. Thank you.' Mr Scorpe swept off his great spectacles. 'And could you tell us, doctor, what are the special characteristics shown by a person suffering from this, ah . . .' On went the spectacles again, but just long enough to consult notes. '. . . this, ah, Grosserbayer's Syndrome?'

Dr Heineman bowed. 'Of course!' He prepared to make a count of his fingers. 'One—he will hev drobbles controllink the belence . . .'

'Trouble controlling his balance, yes.'

'. . . particularly in moments of striss or enkziety. At such times. You see? Two—very probably he will hev parapsychotic re-ektions to sixual stimuli. Three—a well-ricogniced symptom of Grosserbayerism is the patient's euphoric, I could even say halucinaaaatory, estimaaaation of his own physical potintial.'

Mr Scorpe silently digested this for some seconds before attempting a translation.

'In other words, doctor, the unfortunate man not only would lack what we sometimes call moral control, but would have an exaggerated idea of his own vitality?'

'Igsectly! But igsectly!'

'So might it not be fair to say that a man suffering from this, ah, most distressing condition would be less, far less, responsible for his actions than if he was not thus afflicted?'

'Ye-e-es, I might egree with thet—within certain limits, you unterstend. . . .'

Scorpe's spectacles swung upwards to scythe off any qualifications that might have been on their way.

'*If* you please. Now, doctor, one more question only. Are the symptoms of Grosserbayer's Syndrome sufficiently obvious and well-defined for the condition to be diagnosed without undue difficulty?'

The pathologist grinned indulgently at such lawyerly innocence.

'My dear sir! A men sufferink Grosserbayerism is es

obwiaus es . . . a droken policeman—if the inspector will pardon the igsprission. Even the most incompetent —but yes!—in*com*petent general prectice fellow could not fail to see it.'

'*If* you please.' Mr Scorpe sat down. He looked well satisfied.

Purbright wondered if Malley had not slightly underestimated the intentions of the Winge family. Their solicitor certainly was here to put what whitewash he could on the late alderman. But not only that, surely. He was looking for a scapegoat. It was not in the tradition of the Winges to suffer the results of their own actions if someone else could be made to pay.

The deputy coroner indicated to Dr Heineman that he was now free to leave. He did so in high humour and with almost athletic dispatch.

'And now, Dr Meadow: you also have other matters to attend to, I dare say. You are under no obligation to offer evidence unless you think it will help the inquiry. Do you wish to be sworn?'

Dr Meadow, looking round dubiously, was caught in the iron regard of Widow Winge. He shrugged and accepted the testament from Sergeant Malley.

The deputy coroner began his questions. He felt rather proud of having overcome his initial nervousness and was even playing with the pleasant idea of making Meadow look a fool.

'How long had Mr Winge been a patient of yours, doctor?'

'Oh, many years. Perhaps twenty or more.'

'You are, in fact, the family physician?'

'That is so.'

'Had you, in general, considered him a fairly healthy man?'

'With minor exceptions, yes.'

'Right up to the time of his death?'

'He exhibited no symptoms of serious illness.'

'How serious, Dr Meadow, would you consider the condition defined by the last witness as the Grosserbayer Syndrome?"

'That would depend on context.'

'Very well—in the context of Mr Winge, then.'

'I am not convinced that it would be proper to divulge findings arrived at in the privacy of a consulting room.'

'You have *heard* of the Grosserbayer Syndrome, doctor?'

'I think I may say that I am as familiar with the condition as you are, doctor.'

'In that case, I need not ask you if you pursued the appropriate medical regimen.'

'You need not.'

'Did Mr Winge lately complain specifically of having difficulty in keeping his balance?'

'As I have indicated already, I am not prepared to divulge professional confidences.'

'As you wish, doctor. May I put this to you, then? Were you surprised to hear Dr Heineman refer to the symptom of imbalance in connection with Mr Winge's complaint?'

'I should be surprised by nothing Dr Heineman saw fit to propound. Whether I agreed with it or not is quite another matter.'

'There is one further question which it is my duty to ask you, Dr Meadow. Was Mr Winge undergoing —to your knowledge—any form of medication at the time of his death?'

'He was.'

'Of what kind?'

'I am not prepared to say.'

The deputy coroner regarded him narrowly. 'I could press this matter, you know, doctor.'

Meadow said nothing.

The deputy coroner looked at Purbright, who shook his head, and then at Mr Scorpe.

Scorpe lumbered portentously to his feet and glared through his spectacles at a corner of the ceiling as though he had just discovered there the fugitive conscience of Dr Meadow.

"You have, ah, told the court . . .' he began, slowly.

'Mr Scorpe . . .'

It was the deputy coroner speaking.

'Mr Scorpe, I do not have to remind you, of course, that while you are entitled to ask the witness questions, those questions must be simple requests for relevant information. You must not cross-examine. This is not a court of law.'

'*If* you please.' Scorpe bowed with exaggerated humility, then stood for a while nibbling the sidepieces of his occular ordnance.

Suddenly he directed at Meadow a broad, conciliatory smile.

'You have always enjoyed, doctor, have you not, the full confidence and warm appreciation of the Winge family?'

Meadow tried not to look surprised. 'Why, yes, I believe that to be so.'

'And in treating my late client, whose death we all deplore, you invariably employed the full extent of your professional knowledge and skill. . . .' Aloft went Mr Scorpe's glasses to forestall reply. 'No, no, doctor —I require no confirmation. That was a statement, not a question. A statement of known fact.' Mr Scorpe glanced sternly at the deputy coroner, then smiled once more upon Dr Meadow.

'Would you not agree, doctor,' he went on, 'that the family of my late client has offered no objection at any time to the course of treatment you saw fit to prescribe for Alderman Winge?'

'No objection. Not at any time, Mr Scorpe.'

'Of course not!' Scorpe again treated the deputy coroner to a glance of contempt. Dr Thompson scowled back, then ostentatiously consulted his watch.

A piece of paper had appeared in Mr Scorpe's hand. He resumed his fond contemplation of Dr Meadow.

'They did not object—they had, indeed, no known reason to object—to your prescribing a substance named'—Scorpe peered at the paper—'beta-aminotetrylglutarimide?'

There was a moment's silence, perhaps in tribute to Mr Scorpe's feat of pronunciation, then Dr Meadow said carefully:

'I am not in the habit of consulting my patients' relatives, but, as you rightly say, there was no reason why they should have objected. Laymen have no business either to approve or disapprove the prescription of drugs. They know nothing about them.'

'The medical profession, on the other hand, knows *all* about them?'

'I personally make no claim to omniscience.'

'Not in regard to, ah . . . beta-aminotetrylglutarimide?'

'It is a carefully tested and widely approved preparation.'

'How carefully tested, doctor?'

For the first time, Dr Meadow's bearing of dignified condescension showed signs of disturbance. He turned to the deputy coroner.

'I really cannot submit to this line of questioning on medical matters by a lay advocate. It is most improper.'

Dr Thompson, who had been enjoying the exchange between Meadow and Scorpe, made a noncommittal pout.

'If Mr. Scorpe,' added Dr Meadow, 'is intent upon attaching sinister significance to every pill and powder taken by a man who has had the misfortune to fall into a reservoir, I suggest he looks into his late client's devotion to *self*-medication.'

The solicitor made a gesture of huge reasonableness.

'By all means, doctor. Provided, of course, I am so invited by the learned coroner.'

Dr Thompson frowned. The description smacked of irony—but so did all descriptions in the mouth of the impossible Mr Scorpe.

'What had you in mind, doctor?' he asked, quietly.

'Well, not to put too fine a point on it, Winge indulged in quack remedies. I advised against them, naturally, but he tended to be headstrong in these matters.'

'Quack remedies?'

'Yes. Herbs—that sort of thing. His latest addiction, if I am not mistaken, was to something he called "Samson's Salad". He obtained supplies of it by mail order. Looked like compost.'

Purbright heard behind him a hoarse, indignant whispering. He looked round. Old Mrs Crunkinghorn was protesting about something or other to her neighbour, Fireman Hackett.

'May we have quiet, please!' commanded the deputy coroner, feeling by now thoroughly authoritative and ready to slap an odd witness or two into gaol for contempt if he got half a chance.

The disturbance died. Dr Thompson returned his attention to Dr Meadow.

' "Samson's Salad", did you say, doctor? How very odd. Still, it is scarcely within the scope of this inquiry to speculate on the hypothetical effects of some hear-say vegetable. If Mr Scorpe has exhausted his catechism, I don't think we need detain you any longer from your practice.'

Taking great care to look neither grateful nor relieved, Dr Meadow strolled casually from the court.

'And now, perhaps we should hear what Miss Bertha Pollock can tell us. Will you kindly call Miss Pollock, sergeant.'

CHAPTER EIGHT

Dead by misadventure. A poor sort of end for a member of fifteen committees. And yet precisely the same verdict would have been recorded on a famous explorer who had tumbled off a mountain peak. Not death by adventure. Perhaps that would sound too much like approval. No—*mis*adventure.

Inspector Purbright, a few minutes early for an interview the next day with the Chief Constable, beguiled the time by thinking up as many as he could of Alderman Winge's distinguished precursors. General Gordon . . . Casabianca . . . Custer . . . Donald Campbell . . . Shelley. . . .

'Ah, there you are, Mr Purbright.'

'Yes, sir.'

'What's all this they tell me about poor old Steven Winge? Shocking business.'

Mr Chubb laid his bowler hat carefully on the corner of his desk, peeled his gloves into it, and walked over to the fireplace.

'No, sit down, Mr Purbright, sit down.'

The inspector did so.

'It seems that we can dispense with the special night patrols now, sir. I think we've heard the last of the Flaxborough Crab.'

Mr Chubb frowned. 'I do wish the newspapers would not coin these offensive catchwords. Mr Winge may have fallen from grace, as it were, but he had a very distinguished record, you know.'

'Well, versatile, certainly,' said Purbright, rather daringly.

The Chief Constable seemed not to hear.

'I've just been to a Rotary lunch, and Winge's name did crop up in the course of conversation, as you might imagine. He'll be missed, naturally.'

'No doubt, sir.'

'Very nasty for his wife, too, poor soul.'

The inspector did not look convinced. 'My impression at the inquest was that she's a very strong-minded woman. I think she'll live this down quite quickly—possibly with the help of an action for damages against Dr Meadow.'

'Good gracious me! Whatever for? Against Meadow, you say?'

'Scorpe was representing her. And his questions to Heineman and Meadow were extremely pointed. I should say that Scorpe hopes to prove—or to suggest strongly enough to impress a court—that Winge's behaviour was caused by his doctor's faulty prescribing.'

'But that's a very long shot, surely? As I understand it, people only sue doctors for leaving scissors and things inside them. Not for giving them medicine.'

'It depends on the nature of the medicine, sir. Mr Scorpe hinted that the drug given to Winge had not been properly tested and that Meadow didn't know what effects it might have.'

'Ah, well, that is Meadow's worry, not ours. These patrols, Mr Purbright—you're quite happy about our dropping them now, are you?'

'Aren't you, sir?'

'Oh, certainly—so long as you are convinced that poor Winge was responsible for all those unfortunate incidents.'

'I think there can be no reasonable doubt, sir. The behaviour pattern was identical in every case.'

'You don't think you ought to check back, as it were? Check each incident, I mean, against Winge's availability at the time?'

Purbright recognized in the suggestion one of those fairly rare instances of Mr Chubb's choosing to show himself much more intelligent than most people thought. Nevertheless, he shook his head.

'The man will not be accused officially of any of these things, sir, so there is no question of a miscarriage of justice. In any case, reluctance to speak ill of the dead is very strong in a place like Flaxborough—as you must have noticed yourself, sir. Loyalty of that kind does tend to make memories somewhat unreliable.'

The Chief Constable, Rotarianly sensible of what Purbright was getting at, made no comment.

'Even the living are spared on occasion,' Purbright added. 'You may remember, sir, what the girl Brenda Sweeting said about the man who attacked her. She was sure that Dr Meadow could have identified him. I think so, too. I think he recognized Alderman Winge, an old and valuable patient, whom he let go and pretended later not to have seen.'

'Ah, but we cannot make an accusation of that kind, Mr Purbright. Not without incontrovertible proof. Compounding a felony. . . . Well, I mean that is what it would amount to.'

'Yes, it would, sir,' said Purbright, simply. 'And I

don't think it's too harsh a name for behaviour that was calculated to put more women in danger.'

'Perhaps it is as well,' said Mr Chubb, after some thought, 'that things took the turn they did. Strange, how these little mishaps sometimes prove to be blessings in disguise.'

The inspector rose. 'If there's nothing else, sir. . . .'

'No, nothing. Thank you very much.'

When Purbright had gone, the Chief Constable sighed and picked up his hat and gloves. Inquests somehow left a musty smell about the place, even in his own cool and quiet office. An hour's gardening before tea would be rather nice. He put on his hat and gave it a pat in the very middle of its crown. Yes. One hour. Just what the doctor ordered.

The inspector, too, went home earlier than usual. He was not a gardening man, or at least, not compulsively so, but he felt he had earned a little extra leisure.

So did Sergeant Love. He left the police station five minutes before six o'clock and treated himself to a good long look into every shop window on the way home, in particular that of Kumfihomes, on South Gate, where bedroom suites sang siren songs of the Good Life.

Sergeant Malley, for once not having old Albert Amblesby to dispose of, cleared up in record time such matters as filing depositions, obtaining a burial certificate for the undertaker, and reminding the deputy coroner to shell out Dr Heineman's fee. By half-past five, he was watching with keen anticipation the slicing of six ounces of home-cured ham that he was buying from "Trotter" Hamble's in Cromwell Lane to take home for his tea.

Celebration, in fact, was in the air. Nothing wild,

nothing that would have offended the high moral principles of the man whose demise had occasioned it. It was simply a sense of sober satisfaction in the solution of a mystery and the abatement of a dangerous nuisance. Rarely enough are policemen the beneficiaries of the strokes of fate. They generally have to clear up after them. But here, everyone agreed, was one little providential side-swipe that had saved them a lot of trouble.

That night, detectives Pook and Harper, constables Wilkinson and Burke, and their comrades of the Crab-catching Patrol, all slept thankfully and well.

And to an unmarried schoolteacher, alone in the bedroom of her bungalow in Darlington Gardens, there appeared—but not in a vision—a man of mature years who wore no trousers. She dropped her book, screamed, and leaped out of bed to close the curtains. Reaching the window, she saw that the man was already in flight across the lawn. He scuttled towards the back gate in a singularly ungainly manner and disappeared sideways into the lane beyond. A moment later, she heard the starting of a car engine. As she went round the house satisfying herself that all its doors and windows were secure, she wondered if she should dress and telephone the police from the call-box at the end of the road. It seemed pointless now. Instead, she made a cup of hot malted milk, went back to bed, and stayed stubbornly awake until dawn. At half-past nine, she rang the inquiries bell at Fen Street police headquarters and asked by name for Inspector Purbright, whom she once had met, and rather liked, at a school sports day.

He welcomed her with a warmth that was occasioned as much by his still lively appreciation of Alderman Winge's cooperative departure as by the sight of an attractive and sensible-looking young woman.

That was before he heard what she had come to tell.

Even as her story unfolded, he tried to persuade himself that here was some maidenly delusion, born of classroom anxieties and stimulated by wishful thinking. Then he recalled that the schools were on holiday and that, in any case, the desires of so presentable and self-assured a girl were hardly likely to fasten upon an un-trousered ancient. No, what she was describing had unquestionably occurred.

A freakish coincidence, then? An isolated event, quite unrelated to the spate of attacks with which the late alderman had so confidently been credited? One could but hope.

But then came the girl's clearly drawn picture of that now all-too-familiar locomotion of flight—disjointed, crazy, crablike. Purbright groaned inwardly and surrendered to the facts.

Unless it was the ghost of Alderman Winge that had tumbled across a lawn and driven away by car, the police were now faced with the awesome probability of having to capture not one Flaxborough Crab, but several. And there was not a worthwhile clue to the identity of any of them. Not even the Chief Constable, Purbright reflected, could be so madly sanguine as to expect them all to plunge into a reservoir.

He thanked his caller, tried to give her the assurance that he was so far from feeling himself, and saw her out. Then he descended to the C.I.D. room with the intention of breaking the bad news to Love.

Love, though, had troubles already. They were being unloaded by a small, dark-eyed, elderly woman with an expression of resolute gloom. From the sergeant's loud articulation, Purbright judged her to be somewhat deaf.

Spotting the inspector's diffident approach, Love introduced the woman as Mrs Grope.

'The lady is having trou-ble with her hus-band,' he explained at unnecessary volume.

'Oh, yes?'

Mrs Grope seized Purbright's sleeve. 'I'm having trouble with Mr Grope.'

'What sort of trouble, madam?'

She looked inquiringly at Love, as if asking him to waive copyright.

'It seems he's been pestering her a bit lately,' said the sergeant.

Mrs Grope nodded. 'He's forever on about his conjuggling rights. That's not like Mr Grope. It's not his way. I don't know what's come over him.'

'If you mean what I think you mean, Mrs Grope, I really don't think this is a matter in which it would be right for the police to interfere. What did you have in mind to ask us to do?'

'Well, he's taking something, you see.'

Love again intervened.

'She says her husband is taking some sort of a herbal mixture. She thinks it's having an effect on him.'

'It's herbs,' said Mrs Grope. 'I've brought along a packet for you to look at.'

From the depths of a great leather patchwork shopping bag she drew out a green envelope, rather tattered but still bearing a legible yellow label.

Purbright smoothed it out on the table. The label bore, in whimsical woodcraft type, the words SAMSON'S SALAD. Smaller print beneath announced: "A Product of Moldham Meres Laboratories. Prepared from the Genuine Lucky Fen Wort. The Secret of the Amazing Virility of Boadicea's Warriors. Dissolves Instantly."

When the inspector spoke again, his air of polite indifference had changed.

'Tell me, Mrs Grope—in what way has your husband's behaviour been worrying you?'

'Well, several ways. He's not really been himself since we moved to Flax when he left the pictures. . . .'

Interpreter Love quickly scotched the image of Walter Grope, film star.

'He was commissionaire at that cinema in Chalmsbury,* remember. The Rialto. Retired last year.'

Purbright did remember. Grope the rhyming doorman. Big, ponderous and harmless—if one expected teetotalism and an inordinate capacity for versifying. Poor old Grope. Bingo had done for him, as for so many of those splendidly apparelled foyer field-marshals, captains of the queues. . . .

'Yes, of course,' Purbright said. 'I met your husband a year or two back.'

'He's not the same man now,' said Mrs Grope. 'Oh, I don't just mean this conjuggling rights business. I can deal with that. But it's the other things. Just look what I found in the boot cupboard the other morning.'

She pulled from her bag a multi-coloured bundle and thrust it into Purbright's lap, where it unfurled into a miscellany of pairs of knickers.

'Where did he get *them,* I'd like to know!'

'Where, indeed,' murmured Purbright, much impressed.

'From clothes lines, I should think,' Love said, after looking critically at some of the garments. He glanced at the inspector and lowered his voice. 'There have been reports.'

Purbright put the clothing in a heap on the table.

* In *Bump in the Night.*

'You'd better let the policewoman take charge of these for the time being,' he told Mrs Grope. 'Now is there anything else you feel you ought to tell us?'

She pondered darkly.

'He stays out very late some nights.'

'How late?'

'Oh, eleven and after. Once it was nearly one in the morning.'

'Doesn't he tell you where he's been?'

'Pardon?'

'Where he's been. Does he tell you?'

'Never ask.'

'I see. All right. Anything else, Mrs Grope?'

'Well, just that business with the woman in the supermarket.'

'Oh?'

'He's supposed to have interfered with her behind the Shredded Wheat, but there was only her word against his and I'd never known him do that before.'

'Ah, well we mustn't make too much of it, then, must we?' Purbright, hating himself, gave Mrs Grope a reassuring smile. 'I wonder,' he said, 'if it might not be a good idea to have a word with his doctor?'

She shook her head. 'He's not a man you can talk to, Dr Meadow isn't. Very proud. Mr Grope sees him once a week, regular, but *I* won't go. Not to him.'

'Never mind—why don't you talk things over with your husband and persuade *him* to ask the doctor for advice? You don't really want him to be in trouble with the law, I'm sure.'

Purbright cast a worried glance at the heap of underclothes and hoped that their assorted owners would not complicate his life further by positively identifying them. Larceny charges were the last things he wanted to be bothered with at the moment.

Love saw Mrs Grope out. He returned to find the inspector with an unwontedly wild look in his eye.

'My God, Sid! The whole bloody town's infested with sexual maniacs! What the hell are we going to do?'

The sergeant, who could not remember ever before having received so direct a plea for his opinion, did his best to convey an impression of urgent intelligence.

Purbright patted his shoulder.

'Look, before we try and organize anything else, I think we should try and find out all we can about two factors that are common to the only people we've so far been able to connect with this business. Meadow's practice is one factor—both Winge and Grope were his patients. And the second is the stuff in that packet.'

'Did Winge take it as well, then?'

'Meadow said so at the inquest.'

Love held the envelope open and sniffed.

'Smells like lawn clippings.'

'You notice where it's made.'

'Moldham Meres, I suppose. Queer sort of place to find laboratories.'

'I fancy,' said Purbright, 'that "laboratories" will turn out to be huts. Or one hut. Pretentious terms are the very breath of commerce nowadays, Sid.'

'The only sign of life I ever saw out there was a postman taking a short cut from Strawbridge to Moldham Halt.'

'Oh, you do know that part of the world, then?'

Love confessed to having an aunt at Strawbridge whom he visited occasionally.

'In that case, you may mix business with pleasure tomorrow and see what you can learn about Moldham Meres Laboratories. Tactfully, of course. Perhaps your aunt will be able to give you a start. People in country districts are very well informed.'

Purbright looked about him. 'Where's Harper?'

'Probably in the canteen. Shall I find him for you?'

Detective Harper having been traced and summoned, the inspector entrusted him with the surveillance until further notice of Mr Grope.

'Not all the time, you know. I doubt if he will get up to anything during daylight. But watch for him going out in the evening and keep him in sight until he gets back home again. If he does anything really naughty, pull him in, naturally.'

'Mind you,' Purbright confided to Love when Harper had gone, 'I can't imagine dozy old Walter as a rapist, somehow. The trouble is that we can't be sure of anybody any more. Something or other is sending half the over-sixties round the twist. Until we know what it is and who's behind it, there's precious little we can do.'

The sergeant was examining again the packet left by Mrs Grope. He moistened the tip of his little finger and touched the powdery grey-green contents. Then, very cautiously, he licked the grains that had stuck to the finger end. Eyes closed, he made rabbity little movements with his mouth, then remained quite still for several seconds as if hopeful of a Dracula-like transformation. The only outcome, however, was a sneeze.

'Bless you,' said Purbright.

CHAPTER NINE

The door of Dr Meadow's house was opened by a girl of about eighteen who wore upon her head something white and lacy. Purbright's first thought was that the girl was a patient, visiting the doctor in his off-hours, and that the white object was a lightweight bandage of some kind. But would a patient say 'Good morning, sir' and just stand there?

He realized with something of a shock that the bandage was in fact what used to be called a "maid's cap" (he had last seen one on a café waitress in Bournemouth in 1949) and that the girl was a domestic servant.

'Is the doctor at home?'

'I'll just go and see, sir.'

'But don't you know?' (The house couldn't be all that big.)

She reddened and he was sorry to have embarrassed her.

'I'll see, sir,' she said again.

After a while, he heard someone cry 'Yes?' It sounded impatient, hostile. From a doorway down the hall the face of Mrs Meadow looked out. She kept the rest of herself out of view. (Bad payer, thought Purbright.)

He called to her, genially. 'Good morning, Mrs Meadow.'

No sign of recognition. 'Yes? What is it you want? Who are you?'

He wanted very much to bellow: *I am a* DEBT COLLECTOR, *madam!* but restrained himself.

'We have met, Mrs Meadow. I am (up, irresistibly, went his voice, after all) A POLICE INSPECTOR. Purbright is my name.'

On the announcement of his dreadful vocation, at a pitch that might just have reached the nearest neighbours, Mrs Meadow emerged like a flushed-out stoat and hastened to the front door.

'All right, what is it you want?'

'I wish to speak to your husband. Is he available?'

'Couldn't you have seen him at the surgery? It is not convenient for him to be disturbed at home.'

'I am not here for a consultation, Mrs Meadow. Not as a patient, anyway. If the doctor would prefer to come and see me, I dare say it could be arranged.'

Mrs Meadow was looking very annoyed indeed, yet curiously impotent, as if at a loss to know how to keep in his place someone with whom there was no financial relationship.

'Perhaps you had better come in. I'll see if he can spare a minute.'

She stepped back and he came in past her. She shut the door and walked away up the hall.

Invited neither to follow nor to wait in any of the other rooms, Purbright stood patiently and looked around.

He saw a heavy mahogany coat-stand, with mirror and two brushes and a desk-like compartment, presumably for gloves. The hat pegs were antelope horns. No hats hung there; no coats either. The whole affair was kept scrupulously polished, though.

Set against the opposite wall was a semi-circular table. Three letters lay on it. A small tray. Silver?—no, plate, but a good one. For bearing cards, no doubt. *A gentleman to see you, sir. . . .* Oh, and a gong! Heavens, a nine-inch brass gong, complete with a wash-leather striker, on its own little stand. Sid would love that.

He looked at the pictures. There were a dozen or more, set in a straight line at eye level. The subjects were random: a water-mill, the Haymarket Theatre in 1905, a school tennis group, Degas ballet girls. Yet the frames were uniform. Mrs Meadow's arrangement, no doubt.

'Inspector! You mustn't stand around like that. Why haven't you made yourself comfortable?'

Meadow was twenty or thirty feet away, but his voice filled the hall. He was wearing a suit of oatmeal-coloured tweed. He looked much taller than when Purbright had seen him last, longer in the leg and arm. His face was pinker, his manner more boomingly genial. Purbright thought perhaps he had been alarmed by his wife's rudeness and was trying to make amends.

A door was being thrust inward. 'Come along in, there's a good chap.'

The room was less spacious than that in which the inspector had seen Brenda Sweeting, but more richly decorated. A Regency couch and four matching chairs were spaced in a precise pattern, like a group in a furniture museum. Their upholstery, a brocade striped in gold and pale blue, was of brochure brightness. The walls were covered in what looked like chamois suede, embossed with a lozenge motif. Stark white moulding encompassed a ceiling of crystal prisms and drops, frozen on golden wires. A small rosewood writing table stood before the tall window. This was fashioned in a single bow of glass, through which Purbright saw smooth lawn and the blue, aseptic gleam of a swimming pool beyond.

Meadow indicated a chair facing the window. Purbright sat. The chair's padding was much harder than he had expected. Meadow lowered himself carefully upon the couch and leaned forward, clasping his hands, ready to be consulted.

'I am a good deal bothered,' the inspector began, 'by a problem which I am coming to think might be as much in your province as in mine. You know what I am talking about, I suppose?'

'I would rather you were more specific. Guesswork is not good medicine.'

'Very well, doctor. Let us start with the young girl who was attacked in the road outside here, although that was not really the beginning—there were earlier cases of a similar kind. You do know that there have been several such attacks. Almost an epidemic, in fact.'

Meadow nodded pleasantly. 'So I understand.'

'These cases have certain common features. Let me tell you what they are. Firstly, the attacker invariably is described as elderly. Secondly, he seems to be of middle-class background. What little he has been heard to say suggests that he is not uneducated or inarticulate. Also he dresses fairly soberly and is likely to own a car.

'Thirdly—and this is where we enter your field, doctor—the man has a quite extraordinary propensity for losing his sense of balance. Every witness has remarked on the way he runs. "Sideways" is how they all describe it.'

Meadow shrugged. 'Inner ear trouble,' he said. 'Not uncommon.'

Purbright regarded him for a moment.

'At the inquest of Steven Winge,' he said, 'the pathologist said something about a syndrome—I can't remember the name he put to it. He talked of a disturbance of the central nervous system, didn't he?'

'I am not a neurologist, inspector.'

'But that was how he phrased it, was it not?'

'As far as I recall, yes.'

'Thank you. I am going to be perfectly frank with you, doctor. When we learned the circumstances of old Winge's death, we felt reasonably confident that it was he who had been responsible for all the recent attacks on women in this town. And the medical evidence seemed to confirm that opinion. Yet within hours of his death, a young and intelligent woman reported an incident which tallied in every detail with the sort of thing that had been going on before. She described having watched the man run away. Sideways, of course. You see where that leaves us?'

'I see that you would seem to owe poor old Winge an apology.'

'Well, not quite. It cannot be denied that he made a very determined attack on Miss Pollock. He might well have given in to similar impulses recently. But what is now certain—and very disturbing—is that there is someone else, perhaps several other people, given to the same kind of behaviour. And he, or they, must be found.'

'A very proper sentiment, inspector. I hope you are successful.'

'Oh, we shall be. Eventually.'

'Good.'

Meadow looked at his watch, which was gold, very slim but of large diameter, and worn on the inside of the wrist so that he had to make an elegant gesture with his hand in order to see its face. He half rose.

Purbright was staring gravely out of the window.

'I think you could, if you wished, help to shorten the time it is going to take to clear this business up.'

The doctor sat again and leaned back, frowning.

'In what way?'

'For one thing, I was hoping that you would tell me—in confidence and off the record—what the condition was for which you were treating Alderman Winge.'

'I was asked that question at the inquest.'

'And you declined to answer.'

'A doctor has every right to resist probes into his professional relationship with a patient.'

'An inquest is a public hearing. That did make your position difficult, sir. This is a private—and, I hope, friendly—talk. The patient is dead. Do you not think that ethics might be slightly relaxed?'

Meadow saw the inspector's faint smile. 'Yes, but even so . . .' He hesitated.

'You have seen the post-mortem report.'

'Of course.'

'You could tell me if it squared with your knowledge of Winge's condition.'

'Heineman has certain bees in his bonnet. Some of his interests are rather obscure.'

'The what's-its-name syndrome, for instance?'

'That, yes. I have said that I am not a neurologist. If I have a special field, it is geriatrics.'

'Treatment of the old?'

'You could call it that. Winge was getting on. Active, but getting on. I prescribed accordingly.'

'Tonics—that sort of thing.'

'Well, the modern equivalent. Vitality is quite easily

regulated nowadays by an appropriate drug regimen. The process is well proven.'

'Is there no danger of such drugs having unwanted effects?'

Meadow laughed. 'You must beware of popular superstition, inspector. The very word "drug" still conjures up visions of opium dens. But any medicinal substance is, by definition, a drug.'

'These particular medicinal substances, then—can they not operate harmfully in certain circumstances? By overdose, say?'

'Every drug has side effects that are undesirable in greater or lesser degree. Every single one. It is a matter of balancing good against bad. Would you rather have polio than risk vaccination rash?'

'No, what I am driving at . . .'

'What you are driving at, inspector, is this—and correct me if I am wrong—Was I prescribing something for Mr Winge that turned him into a randy old goat?'

The inspector looked pleased.

'Ah, now we are getting near the nub of the matter. May I phrase the question more delicately? Was there any possibility to Mr Winge over-doing his treatment—taking too many tablets, capsules or whatever—and thus stepping up his vitality to a degree that might land him in trouble?'

'None whatever. I know you do not mean to imply irresponsible prescribing, so I shall not read into your remarks as much as I might. But let me put your mind at rest, Purbright. The treatment I considered necessary for Mr Winge was strictly controlled on a week-to-week basis. That is my invariable practice. It is also a rule of mine—and of other doctors, I do not doubt—to make use only of such drugs as have been subjected to exhaustive clinical trial and are manufactured by a reputable house. I might add that in my own field of geriatric medicine I have done some contributory work on the clinical side—work that has received recognition rather farther afield than you might think. I am not likely to put at hazard either my patients or my reputation by taking the slightest risk of any kind you seem to have had in mind.'

It was a speech of reproof and dismissal, and Purbright was not misled by the amiable tone of Meadow's cultured, beautifully modulated voice into hoping that he might gain from the interview.

But perversely he tried.

'The man who assaulted Brenda Sweeting—have you no idea of his identity?'

'None.'

'Could he possibly have been Alderman Winge?'

'I did not see his face.'

'But can you assert definitely that it was *not* Winge? As a patient, he must have been familiar to you.'

'That possibility did not occur to me at the time. Why should it? My only concern was to save the girl further distress. Once he had run away, the obvious thing to do was to make sure she had not been injured.'

'Do you happen to know a man called Walter Grope, doctor?'

If the switch of subject surprised Meadow, he gave no sign.

'Grope?' he repeated levelly. 'I do have a patient named Grope. Walter, though . . . I couldn't be sure without checking.'

'A man of sixty-odd. He moved here recently from Chalmsbury. A retired cinema commissionaire.'

'I believe he is, yes. What about him?'

'I have advised his wife to have a talk with you about him. His behaviour has been worrying her.'

'Behaviour? What sort of behaviour?'

'Something, I gather, along the same lines as Mr Winge's little weakness. An excess of vitality.'

'You surely cannot expect me to comment on that, inspector. If Mrs Grope sees fit to seek my professional advice, that is up to her. I cannot discuss with you or anyone else some hypothetical marital problem that even my own patient has not mentioned.'

'The problem might not be purely marital,' said Purbright. 'The law could well become involved.'

'Ah.'

Meadow rose to his feet. He walked in his easy, athletic way to the window and looked out, his hands clasped loosely behind him.

'As to that,' Purbright heard him say, 'I should prefer to hear no more, if you wouldn't mind. It is the physical welfare of my patients that concerns me, not their relations with the law.'

'Crime concerns us all, doctor—if you will forgive the triteness of the sentiment.'

Meadow turned to face the room.

'Policemen,' he remarked pleasantly, 'do not have a monopoly of social conscience. When next I see Mr Grope committing a crime, I shall assuredly remonstrate with him. All right?'

He stepped to the door. The smile he directed upon the inspector was as warm as a car salesman's.

Purbright stood. He glanced behind him at the chair. Its splendid satin had regained its creaseless convexity.

'I hope you haven't found my intrusion too tiresome, Dr Meadow.'

'My dear chap! What an idea!'

One slender, immaculately clean hand was drawing

open the door. The other was extended in a gesture at once courteous and peremptory. (He's a great one for showing out, Purbright said to himself.)

The inspector was almost through the doorway when he stopped suddenly, looked at Meadow, snapped his fingers and said: 'Salad.'

Bewilderment—a very rare visitor to the doctor's handsome and confident features—was certainly upon them now.

'Salad,' Purbright said again. 'Samson's Salad. I nearly forgot to ask you about that.'

Meadow shrugged, apparently still doubtful of what Purbright was talking about.

'At the inquest, you spoke of Winge's indulgence in self-medication. You mentioned a specific herbal preparation. Wasn't that its name? Samson's Salad?'

'Oh, that. Yes, so I understand. Why?'

'What do you know about it?'

'Only that Winge claimed it did him good.'

'You didn't investigate it yourself—have it analysed, or anything?'

'Good lord, no. Patients are always putting that sort of rubbish into themselves. I advised against it, naturally, but I don't suppose he took any notice.'

'Might something of that sort have produced the symptoms we were talking about before? The loss of balance, for instance?'

'Conceivably.'

'Sexual stimulation?'

'Certain vegetable extracts do have that effect. I am not saying that this particular preparation did so.'

'But you saw fit to draw it to the attention of the coroner. And by name. That did rather suggest to me, doctor, that you considered it suspect.'

'I did not want any fact overlooked that might be relevant, that's all.'

'But the coroner did not take up the point.'

'No. I had made it, though. That was enough for me.'

'Certainly. By the way, do you happen to know of anyone else who takes this stuff?'

'I do not.'

'None of your patients—apart from Mr Winge?'

'No.' For the first time, Meadow's manner was unmistakably curt.

Purbright gave a slight bow.

'You've been most tolerant, doctor.'

'Not at all.' Affability was back instantly and in full measure.

Meadow watched the inspector's last commending glance at the room's contents before he turned to leave.

'You are a furniture man, are you Purbright?'

He sounded eager to establish kinship, as with a newly identified club member.

'I am not a collector, if that's what you mean, sir. I find some of it very satisfying to look at, though.'

'I see you're too wise to become acquisitive.'

'No—just too poor.'

As Purbright walked away from the closing front door, he realized that the doctor had considered his final remark to be simply a smart riposte, a piece of policemanlike repartee. Meadow clearly was well-off to that degree at which shortness of cash is an abstraction as imponderable as death.

CHAPTER TEN

Sergeant Love's auntie at Strawbridge was very pleased to see him. She straightened his tie, asked him if he thought his jacket would be warm enough should the weather change, announced that it was a bad year for plums, put her hands over his ears ('My, you *are* cold!') in order to haul his forehead down to kissing distance, and said she thought he ought to eat more.

Having submitted to these affectionate preliminaries and drunk a cup of milky coffee totted up with his aunt's rhubarb brandy, Love asked what she knew of what went on at Moldham Meres these days, particularly in the matter of laboratories.

'Laboratories?'

'That's right. The Moldham Meres Laboratories. That's what they call themselves.'

'You don't mean the old herb farm, do you?'

Love looked doubtful. Despite Purbright's caution, he had hoped for white-coated scientists, toting test tubes against a background of retorts and spiralling lights. The old herb farm, as he recalled it, was an overgrown field containing a decrepit cottage and a couple of sheds.

'There *is* somebody there now,' his aunt persisted. 'The house was done up about a year ago and there's a board outside. I haven't looked close to see what's on it.' She waited a moment. 'Well, there's nothing else at the Meres.'

This, as Love well knew, was no overstatement. It was the herb farm or nothing.

He set off on the two miles walk across country after promising his aunt that he would be back in time to have what she called "a proper meal" before returning to Flaxborough on the afternoon train from Strawbridge.

He enjoyed the walk. By keeping to remembered bridle paths and rights of way around the fields of late, reddish-brown corn, he was able to avoid metalled road altogether until he emerged on the lane leading to Moldham Halt.

On the way, he provided himself with a switch of elder and light-heartedly slashed the tops of nettle and cow parsley as he strode. Have-at-you Love, with all-conquering blade. Zounds. . . . At intervals, he plucked and munched a blackberry.

His aunt had been right. He was still a hundred yards from the cottage when he saw the patches of bright new tile with which the roof had been repaired. From a chimney rose a thin plume of smoke. Some of the creeper on the side facing the road had been cut away to leave the windows clear. The panes were picked out with fresh paint.

Love halted at the new tubular steel gate and looked through.

The field looked unchanged from when he had last seen it. There were no signs of cultivation. The once neat herb beds had long since ceased to be distinguishable. They were overrun with weeds and rank grass, although here and there a great bolted bush of sage or thyme survived as testimony to the place's original use.

Fixed to the cottage wall, at one side of an uncurtained but clean window, was a board with an announcement in slim, pale green lettering on a chocolate ground.

MOLDHAM MERES LABORATORIES: Registered Office.

Love opened the gate and walked down the path to the cottage. There was a door in the gable end. He let fall its horseshoe knocker. It produced an echoing sound suggestive of the house being sparsely furnished. He waited. Nothing happened. He knocked again. No result.

He noticed a little text, lettered in a style and colour-scheme similar to those of the signboard, set in the top panel of the door.

"NATURE—O TRUE APOTHECARY!"

Dinky, Love reflected.

He walked round to the back of the cottage and looked through a window. He saw a big office table on which stood an addressograph, a typewriter and several piles of leaflets, stationery and packets. Two filing cabinets stood against the farther wall.

The next window was that of a small kitchen containing sink, stove and refrigerator. On the table were the remains of a meal.

In the room beyond—the last on this side of the house—the sergeant saw a low divan bed, unmade, a couple of chairs, a gate-leg table and a television set. The floor was carpeted and there were curtains at the window.

Love was still peering into this room when he heard the sudden rising whine of an electric motor, followed by a clattering, grating sound. He turned.

The noise seemed to come from one of three adjoining sheds at the farther side of the paved yard in which he stood. It was a vaguely familiar sound.

After a few moments he placed it. An electric food blender, running on dry ingredients.

The door of the right-hand shed opened and the noise became louder. There emerged a short, thin, wiry, baldheaded man in shirt and trousers. Love saw sunlight flash from a pair of rimless spectacles. The man stood outside the door. He blinked, scratched an ear, yawned, then bent down to stroke a ginger cat that had appeared from round the corner of the shed.

As the man straightened again, he spotted the sergeant. Hastily he stepped back through the doorway.

Half a minute passed. Then he came once more into the sunlit yard, this time with slow dignity. Love was surprised to see that he was now wearing a kind of voluminous brown dressing gown, corded round the waist.

Love stepped to meet the thin man, who nodded gravely and raised two fingers in greeting. (Scoutmaster? wondered the sergeant—no, surely not.)

'Good morning, sir. I am Detective Sergeant Love, from Flaxborough, and I should like to speak to the manager.'

Love believed that straightforward declarations of this kind were more productive in the long run than the clever, pussyfooted approach.

' 'Ow do?' responded the man. He held out his hand. 'Brother Culpepper's the name.'

As he shook hands, Love tried not to show the apprehension that always rose within him whenever involvement with religion threatened. A bloody monk! Surreptitiously, he glanced across the other's shoulder for the sure sign of monkhood, a cowl. Yes, there it was.

'Pleased to meet you, Your, er . . .' (Reverence, was it? Grace?)

'The boss ain't 'ere yet,' said Brother Culpepper. 'I'm on me tod, 'smatterfact. Anyfink I can do for you?'

'Well, I don't quite know. I'm just making some routine inquiries.'

Brother Culpepper looked up at him in friendly wonderment.

'Wot, somebody lost somefink, you mean?'

The chirpy Cockney accent increased rather than diminished Love's respect. A man who could achieve holy orders despite such a social disadvantage must clearly be of the strongest character.

'No, nothing special, really. I just want to check on various things. Food and Drugs Act. You know.'

'Like to see rahnd? I'm the 'erbmaster. Or if you'd rather come back abaht eleven. . . . Christ! I've left them choppers runnin'. . . .'

He darted back into the shed. A few seconds later, the electric blender noise died.

'Sorry abaht that, but they run 'ot if they're left. Nah them, wot was I sayin'?—yeah, if you like to give it an hour, the boss orter be in then. Wotcher fink?'

Love deliberated.

'Well, actually . . . Beg pardon, what was it you said you did here?'

'I'm 'erbmaster.'

'You look after the, er . . .' Love jerked his head towards the sheds.

'Thasright. The 'ole caboodle—'erbs, driers, choppers—the lot.'

'But isn't there anyone else here? Working, I mean.'

'Only young Florrie.'

Brother Culpepper looked at his hands, then gave them a vigorous wipe on a square yard of his robe.

'She comes over three times a week from Moldham

to do the packin' an' that. Then there's the boss, o' course. Office stuff—she does all that. But 'er hours ain't wot you'd call regular, 'cos she's got a long way to come, see.'

'And do you have far to travel?' Love knew of only one monastery and that was twenty miles the other side of Flaxborough.

'Wot, me? I live in. 'erbmasters always live in, mate. There are fings can go wrong. Lots o' fings.'

'Oh,' said Love.

He looked away from the man's bright, upturned face. It reminded him a little of the face of a salesman on Flaxborough market who once had inveigled him into buying a "fuel extender" to increase by forty per cent his motor cycle's mileage performance. It had turned the petrol into a toffee-like substance that had effectively sealed the engine for ever. But this fellow seemed genuine enough. Why should he wear this get-up out here in the middle of nowhere if he wasn't a real monk?

'I've always rather fancied gardening,' Love remarked. 'Nice quiet sort of life.' He hoped he had compensated for the unworthy straying of his thoughts.

'Oh, it's 'eaven,' agreed Brother Culpepper.

He regarded the sergeant carefully for a moment.

'I'm on wot they call release from the Order, see? Sort of lent aht. Abbot's dispensation.'

'Ah,' said Love, nodding.

'Lickewer's really my line, o' course. Chartroose. This makes a change, though.'

'Yes, it must.'

Love gazed past the end shed, trying to discern some area of disciplined cultivation in the wilderness of weeds.

'What is it, exactly, this, er . . . you know—what you make here?'

'Wot *is* it?' echoed Culpepper, incredulously. 'Don't tell me you 'avent 'eard of Lucky Fen Wort?'

'Well, I . . .'

'Balm of Befle'em?'

The sergeant pretended to think hard.

'Samson's Salad?' urged Culpepper. 'Cor, but you *must* 'ave!'

'Oh, that. Yes. Yes, I have.'

'*Course* you 'ave!' The monk puffed his cheeks roguishly and gave Love's chest a flip with the back of his hand.

The sergeant swallowed. 'What is it supposed to do, though? I'm not very well up on herbs.'

At once Culpepper's face was serious and eager once more.

'Look,' he said, 'if I didn't know wot was wot regardin' miracles an' that, I'd say that stuff was one. A miracle. No—straight up, I would.'

'Good, is it?'

'Good? *Good?*' Culpepper's little eyes squeezed to mere creases behind his glasses, then popped. 'It's aht o' this flippin' world, bruvver!'

'You mean it cures things?'

'Har . . .'—Culpepper raised a finger—'as to that, we've got to be careful, 'aven't we, eh? Claims is dodgy fings. I'm not goin' to stand 'ere an' tell you Lucky Fen Wort will cure this and Lucky Fen Wort will cure that. I mean, I know all abaht renderin' under Caesar an' all that. But wot I will say—and may 'E strike me if I tell a lie—'Im, not Caesar, I mean—wot I *will* say is, Lucky Fen Wort didn't get it's name for nuffink.'

The sergeant looked at his watch. The inspector was not going to thank him for having spent an entire morning learning that the promoters of Samson's Salad offered nothing more definite than good luck (the late Alderman Winge's experience notwithstanding).

'This manager of yours—you think she'd be here about eleven.'

'Should be.'

'And what did you say her name was?'

Brother Culpepper hauled up his gown and fished a leather wallet from his trousers pocket. He extracted a pale lilac card and handed it to Love.

'That's 'er.' He pointed to the name in the bottom left corner of the card. 'Luvly lady. Used to be a missionary.'

The sergeant noted that a smile of blissful devotion had appeared on Culpepper's face. He examined the card. Under a delicate floral motif was printed MOLDHAM MERES LABORATORIES, MOLDHAM, ENGLAND . . . Director: Lucilla E. C. Teatime, M.B.E.

Love frowned, but only for a second.

'Is that the Miss Teatime who does the charity work in Flax?'

'Wot! You know 'er?' A beam of surprise and congratulation.

'We have met once or twice.'

'Oh, a luvly lady!'

Love looked again at the card, then slipped it into his pocket. 'I hadn't realized she was an M.B.E.'

'She's a great one for 'iding lights under bushes,' explained Brother Culpepper. He sighed. 'Anyway, p'raps you'd like to come an' 'ave a shufti?'

'A what?'

'A look-see. A stroll rahnd.'

He led Love to the first shed and held the door open for him to enter.

It was very dim inside. There was a cool, earthy smell, overlaid with an aromatic odour that reminded

Love of newly mown road verges. Against one side of the shed had been heaped greenery of some kind, spangled with bright yellow flowers.

'That's the wort 'arvest,' his guide told him. 'It's brought in 'ere an' graded.'

The sergeant saw no evidence of grading. The green stuff lay in one big pile. There were several baskets lying around, though. He stepped between them and picked a sample of the harvest, examining leaves and stalk with what he hoped would look like intelligent appreciation.

'Very like dandelion,' was the only comment that occurred to him.

'Ah,' responded Culpepper immediately, 'yor dead right. Lots o' people can't see the diff'rence. But 'erbs is like everyfink else—you gotta know 'em, see? Takes years.'

He took the sample from Love, sniffed it fastidiously, then slowly split a stem with his thumb nail.

'See?' He indicated the stem's viscous inner surface. 'That's wort orlright.'

He tossed the plant back on the heap and turned towards the door.

In the middle shed, Culpepper pointed to nets stretched from wall to wall on which were spread thin layers of shrivelling leaves.

'Dryin' 'ouse,' he explained.

They went on to the third shed.

The air here was dusty. It smelled, Love thought, rather like the inside of Pearsons' seed warehouse in North Street. This was where the sound of machinery had come from. He saw an electric motor bolted to a table and, nearby, what appeared to be an outsize coffee mill. The mill was surmounted by a hopper. To a delivery pipe at the bottom of the machine a canvas bag, rather similar to a post office sorting bag, had been clipped.

Culpepper tipped the contents of a basket into the hopper and switched on the motor. Above the resultant racket he shouted triumphantly: 'Untouched by 'uman 'and!' and pointed to the canvas bag, which slowly fattened.

On the other side of the gangway was a second table, bearing a big enamelled bowl, a couple of scoops, a kitchen spring balance and a pile of empty packets.

Brother Culpepper walked over to it.

'This is where young Florrie gives an 'and.'

He thrust a scoop into what Lucky Fen Wort had been left in the bowl at the end of Florrie's last shift and yelled:

'Goes all over the flippin' country, this does! Arsk an' it shall be given unto yew!'

Love took this to be a scriptural jest of some sort and grinned sheepishly.

Culpepper stepped back and switched off the motor.

'That's abaht it, then,' he said.

'Very interesting,' said Love. He was wondering what else he could usefully ask when Culpepper picked up his head and listened.

' 'Ello, 'ello, 'ello—'ere comes the Queen of Sheba!'

The sergeant heard the hornet-like crescendo of an approaching car—a sports car, without doubt. He followed Culpepper into the sunlight. Three seconds later, what seemed to be a wheeled projectile, immaculately agleam and pulsating wickedly, drew up before them.

A shoe—brown suede, well cut; a neat ankle and calf, finely stockinged; a skirt low enough to be modest without looking dowdy; a slim yet energetic body, dressed one season in arrear but with that kind of informed taste that makes fashion seem beside the point;

delicate but capable hands, fluttering now to show pleasure; a face that bespoke no particular age despite its innocence of any but the most elementary make-up; gentle, shrewd eyes. . . .

'Sergeant!' One of the finely shaped hands extended in friendliness. 'How delightful to see you again!'

Love grinned and shuffled his feet.

'And how is your Mr Purbright?' asked Miss Teatime, cheerfully.

'He's very well, thank you, ma'am.'

'Do give him my regards.'

She turned to Brother Culpepper, who had been watching the encounter with obvious approval.

'And have you been showing Sergeant Love our little enterprise?'

' 'sright.'

Miss Teatime smiled again at Love.

'What monastic modesty doubtless has prevented his telling you is that Brother Culpepper is our guiding genius out here at Moldham. The church's loss has been our gain. Oh, temporarily, of course—you must not suppose that his Order would part with him for good.'

'I told 'im that. Abaht bein' on loan, like.'

'Would you care for a cup of coffee, sergeant? Then you coud tell me the reason for this very welcome visit.'

She led Love to the cottage and into the room with the addressograph and filing cabinets. They sat on gaunt but quite comfortable steel chairs. Brother Culpepper, whose worldly service apparently extended to the kitchen department, could soon be heard rattling crockery. A couple of minutes later, he brought in a tray and made space for it on the table by elbowing aside some of the packets and labels.

'Back in 'alf 'nour,' he remarked on his way out. 'Be seein' yer.'

'His devotions,' Miss Teatime explained softly to the sergeant. 'We give him all facilities, naturally.'

She poured Love a full cup of the strong coffee-and-milk mixture from a jug and passed him a small sugar bowl. Her own cup she less than half filled, then topped it up with a pale amber fluid from a medicine bottle that she took from the white cabinet, painted with a red cross, on the wall behind them.

'Friar's Balsam,' she said with a little grimace of resignation, putting back the cork. Then, as if by after-thought, she looked inquiringly at Love and held out the bottle. 'But perhaps you, too, are a bronchitis sufferer, sergeant?'

Love hurriedly shook his head and pulled his coffee to safety. It was only later, when he caught a steam-borne whiff of a surprisingly alcoholic nature, that he regretted his conservatism.

Miss Teatime sipped her remedy with considerable fortitude.

'I trust that your call has nothing to do with the more depressing aspect of a policeman's job, Mr Love. It is difficult in the peaceful atmosphere of the country-side to conceive of lawlessness, you know.'

'Well, I can't say that there's any lawlessness in-volved, actually. Mr Purbright just wanted me to have a look and see what was here. He doesn't know it has anything to do with you, I'm sure.'

'Is he interested in herbal therapy, then?'

Love hesitated. 'Well, no, I shouldn't have thought so. The fact is, we've had a bit of trouble in Flax, and this stuff you make here does happen to have been mentioned.'

He blushed and stared into his cup, unhappily aware

of the difficulty of deceiving a lady so well-bred as Miss Teatime.

'But surely'—Miss Teatime looked puzzled—'there can be no suggestion of our product having been concerned in this, ah, trouble? It is altogether wholesome, I assure you.'

'Yes, I'm sure it is. The Reverend seemed to think so, anyway.'

'Brother Culpepper? Oh, yes, his judgment is very sound where the fruits of the earth are concerned. But perhaps you can tell me a little more about your inspector's anxieties?'

Love related the facts of Alderman Winge's death by drowning following his attempted seduction of Miss Pollock and a subsequent attack of giddiness. He repeated the assertion by Dr Meadow at the inquest that Winge had been dosing himself with Samson's Salad, which, Love understood, was synonymous with Lucky Fen Wort, as processed and packaged at the Moldham Meres Laboratories. The sergeant forebore from cataloguing the other cases of indecent assault; nor did he mention Mrs Grope's suspicions concerning association between Fen Wort and the recent disconcerting behaviour of her husband.

Miss Teatime listened to all this with grave and polite attention. Then she replenished his cup and helped herself to a booster shot of Friar's Balsam.

'How very distressing,' she murmured. 'But I am certain that Dr Meadow cannot have meant to blame our Samson's Salad for what happened to his poor patient. Its action is invigorating but not in the least degree harmful. Indeed, I am only surprised—though relieved, naturally—to hear that Mr Winge did not catch the lady he was pursuing.'

'She was a good runner, by all accounts.'

'That is as well.'

There was a short pause.

'Tell me, though, Mr Love—was the criticism by Dr Meadow voiced publicly at the inquest?'

'Oh, yes. He'd been rather nettled by the deputy coroner, as a matter of fact. The inspector seems to think he was trying to put himself in the clear.'

'I see.'

The ensuing silence sharpened a feeling in Love that his appearance at Moldham Meres must look odd and even foolish if he could think of no better justification. He had been received very kindly. Everything here seemed to be above board. Surely Purbright would not blame him for being a little more forthcoming.

He found himself saying: 'Strictly between ourselves . . .'

Miss Teatime leaned forward. She looked concerned and very sympathetic.

'. . . we do have reports of another customer of yours, and it could be that he's the same way inclined as old Winge.'

'Dear me!'

'That's how it looks. Confidentially, of course.'

'Naturally.'

'His wife's very worried. She says he's taken to interfering with women in shops and collecting, well—you know—garments.'

Miss Teatime found the sergeant's propensity for blushing most endearing. She nodded understandingly.

'According to her,' Love went on, 'all this began when he started taking this herb stuff. That's according to her,' he added defensively.

'You are being so agreeably frank, sergeant, that I wonder if you would care to divulge the gentleman's name. I need hardly say that it would go no further.'

'Well . . .' He hesitated.

'Yes?'

'It's Grope, actually.'

Miss Teatime pondered, then shook her head.

'No, I'm afraid the name is not familiar to me.' She smiled. 'Perhaps I had best forget it again. Now then, is there any other matter in which you think I might be able to help you?'

Love thought not, but thanked her for asking.

When he had gone, Miss Teatime opened a drawer in one of the filing cabinets. After a brief search, she tweaked up a card. It was that of the only Grope on the mailing index. She copied the address into her little memorandum book, resumed her seat at the table, and thoughtfully lighted a slim, black cheroot.

CHAPTER ELEVEN

Brother Culpepper re-entered the office some twenty minutes later. When he saw that Miss Teatime was alone, he hauled off his habit and hung it on a hook at the back of the door. Then he slumped into the chair vacated by Sergeant Love and felt in his shirt pocket for a cigarette end and a match. The cigarette end was crumpled and very short. He lit it with his lips pouted well forward and his eyes nearly shut.

'What a nice policeman Sergeant Love is,' remarked Miss Teatime. 'Did you not think so, Joe?'

'Oh, yurs. A right darlin'.' Culpepper hooked his tongue tip round the smouldering butt and shifted it to the opposite corner of his mouth. 'Wot was 'e after, anyway?'

'He was making routine inquiries.'

'They always are. Lot o' ponshus pilots.'

'Now, you must not be unjust, Joe. The sergeant is very helpful. It is not every policeman who gives warning of impending bad publicity.'

'Eh? 'Ow d'yer mean, Looce?'

'It seems that a certain Dr Meadow has been making remarks that cast reflection upon our product. As those remarks were made at an inquest, it is very likely that they will be reported in the Press—in the local Press, at all events. We must hope that his calumnies will not spread further afield.'

'Oo, 'ell!'

Miss Teatime regarded the remnant of her cheroot, then tamped it out scrupulously in an earthenware ashtray.

'Of course,' she said, 'the effects will not necessarily be disastrous. On the one hand, it would be highly beneficial if the story were to gain ground that Lucky Fen Wort puts lead into the pencils of elderly gentlemen. That, after all, is what we have tried to convey in more delicate terms through the advertisement columns.'

'Shoor,' agreed Brother Culpepper. Puckering his face, he sucked a final dividend of smoke from the brown pellet in his mouth corner, then extracted it between finger and thumb and flicked it accurately into the fireplace.

'What would *not* be beneficial,' resumed Miss Teatime, 'is the suggestion by a medical man that our product had contributed not merely to the venal foibles of this Mr Winge but to his death as well. People are very readily swayed by the prejudices of doctors, and they do not like taking things which they fear may kill them.'

'Yurs, but ahr little old Wort 'd never do that.'

'Certainly not. You know and I know and all the good country folk around here know how benign are the remedies of nature. Unfortunately, the professional medical mind admits of no such persuasion.'

'O ye stiff-necked 'ippercrits,' muttered Culpepper. He leaned forward and peered hopefully into the coffee jug, but it was empty.

Miss Teatime got up and walked once or twice from one end of the room to the other.

'There is just one thing which I find extremely puzzling,' she said, halting by the window and looking down into the yard at two cats that lay together and snoozed in the sun. 'Why did our friend Dr Meadow go out of his way to mention Samson's Salad in connection with that man's death? Doctors generally refuse even to acknowledge the existence of what they call quack medicines. His behaviour has been most uncharacteristic. I wonder why.'

Culpepper shrugged.

'The sergeant,' said Miss Teatime, 'used the phrase "trying to put himself in the clear". Clear of what, though? I should love to know.'

'Arst 'im,' suggested Culpepper, raspingly humorous.

Miss Teatime smiled. The smile lingered as she stood in thought.

'No, I have a better idea, Joe. We shall see what Bernie can find out.'

'Bernie?'

'Yes. He is, by the grace of God, still a member of the British Medical Association, is he not?'

'If they ain't rumbled that little old puddin' club clinic of 'is in 'Ampstead, 'e is.'

'Quite. But I have seen no report of his having fallen from favour. I shall make a few preliminary inquiries locally and then telephone Bernie tonight.'

'Knock an' it shall be opened t'yer, me old dear,' quoth Brother Culpepper.

He looked at the clock.

'Nah then, wot's 'appened to that little bugger Florrie this mornin'? We're bunged up wiv bloody Wort til she gets 'ere.'

Miss Teatime discovered that Blackfriars' Court was a sort of nodule on one of the narrow lanes between

Flaxborough Market Place and the river. Enclosing a cobbled area about fifty yards square were four rows of Georgian and early Victorian houses. The houses were quite tall but mostly of only one room's breadth. There was no space between them. They looked like a concourse of widowed sisters, much undernourished and huddled together for comfort.

Only at one spot had they parted company. This was to make way for a Baptist Chapel, a self-satisfied, brick interloper with two imitation campaniles and a rectangular stained glass window. The colours of the glass were neither sombre nor gay, but curiously and unpleasantly provocative. Miss Teatime decided that they had surgical connotations: she noted iodine (for cuts), picric acid (burns), and gentian violet (athlete's foot).

While she was looking, the big imitation gothic doors of the chapel opened and gave birth to a battered sideboard, midwived by two men in white aprons. Miss Teatime recalled that the building was now a second-hand furniture saleroom.

She mounted three steps to the tall, narrow door of number eighteen Blackfriars' Court and knocked. Almost immediately the yellowing lace curtain at the window on her right was edged cautiously aside. She stared resolutely at the knocker, pretending not to notice. Slow, ponderous footsteps echoed on a stone floor within. A bolt grated, then slammed back against its stop. The door opened.

Jumping Christ! said Miss Teatime to herself.

Looming in the shadowy doorway was a man in the uniform of a lieutenant-general of the late Czar's Imperial Russian Army.

For some moments, Miss Teatime's surprise prevented her remembering the formula by which she had planned to gain entrance. But at last she forced her gaze from the ankle-length greatcoat, from the gold braid and the eagle-crested buttons, from the medals and the epaulettes, up to the great grey mournful moon of a face that hung over them. She said:

'Good morning. I am from the Regional Health Insurance Board. Are you Mr Walter Grope?'

The lieutenant-general nodded doubtfully, as if he had not heard the name very often before.

Miss Teatime beamed.

'I wonder if I might come in for a few moments, Mr Grope. A small matter of administrational routine has arisen and I believe you could help us to clear it up.'

'It's not about the tablets, is it?'

Grope sounded as vague as he looked. He had made no move to admit her.

'Tablets?' she repeated, encouragingly.

'The doctor said he was having to stop them.'

'Would that be Dr Meadow, by any chance?'

'He's been on to you people about it, has he?'

'Ah, not directly, no . . .'

Mr Grope absent-mindedly fingered his Order of Vassily (Second Class).

'Perhaps you'd better come through into the room.'

He half-turned, making space for her to pass him, then closed the door.

Miss Teatime paused by the first doorway she came to.

'That's right—in there,' called Mr Grope. She noticed, not unthankfully, that he had neglected to replace the bolt.

The room contained a great deal of furniture, including two pianos, a carved mahogany cupboard the size of a modest bus shelter, an oval dining table draped in port wine-coloured plush, a pedestal gramophone, and a number of formidable sundries that eluded immediate identification.

Miss Teatime picked her way between a piano stool and what she suspected to be a commode, and perched as gracefully as she could upon the arm of a bloated, tapestry-covered settee.

'Yes, these tablets,' she resumed briskly. 'What was it that Dr Meadow told you about them? The fact is that some of our prescription records appear to have gone astray. The question of your tablets might well have a bearing.'

Mr Grope, who had entered the furniture labyrinth by another channel, stared gloomily at her over a bamboo plant stand.

'Doing without them is very wearing,' he declared.

'I am sure it must be, Mr Grope. But what did Dr Meadow say?'

'He didn't hold out any hope. Not when I called on Wednesday.'

Miss Teatime was by no means the first person to have discovered that having conversation with Walter Grope produced a curious sense of being bombarded with echoes. Was it the pianos? she wondered. Reverberations, perhaps.

'Hope of more tablets, do you mean?'

'Of course. They . . .' He paused, made several silent lip movements as if trying out words, then brightened and announced in a rush: 'They-ran-out-on-Tuesday-at-eleven-fif*teen*.'

'That,' observed Miss Teatime, having grasped the reason for the echo effect, 'does not scan.'

'Not really,' Mr Grope agreed.

'But it is very stimulating, if I may say so, to meet someone with so natural a flair for poetry.'

The nearest approximation to a smile of which Mr

Grope was capable stirred momentarily in the featherbed of his cheek.

'Do you compose much verse, Mr Grope?' Miss Teatime inquired, sensible of the perils of the question, but eager to please still further.

'A fair bit. It doesn't come so easy now, though. Not since I finished at the pictures.'

'You were an artist?'

'I was a commissionaire.' Mr Grope flicked an imaginary speck of dust from his splendid sleeve. 'It's an occupation that leaves the mind free for a lot of the time. I used to think up most of my In-Memoriams while I was keeping an eye on the queue at the Rialto.'

'Did you, indeed.'

'For the paper, you know. There was one used to go: *Of all the mothers she was the best—She's gone to where she can get a good rest.*'

'Lovely,' murmured Miss Teatime.

'Then there was: *A dear one's passed, but though we're sad—We know it now is heaven for Dad.* I remember the week I made that one up. It was Gold Diggers of 1933.'

'Films like that will not come our way again, Mr Grope.'

She sighed, then looked at the little silver dress watch that she wore.

'Dear me! The Ministry does not employ me to chatter about old times, I fear. I really must complete these little inquiries of mine and return to the office. Now then, do you by happy chance know the name of the medicine that Dr Meadow had been prescribing for you?'

She took a thin silver propelling pencil from her handbag.

Mr Grope shook his head. For some time, his gaze had been fixed on Miss Teatime's knees.

'I could make a poem about you, if you like,' he said suddenly.

'You cannot remember?'

'The prescription, you mean? Oh, it was just a squiggle. I couldn't make it out.'

'Oh, dear.'

Mr Grope swallowed. He appeared to be working out some kind of a problem. Hopefully, Miss Teatime waited.

'*When beauty like yours I see, my memory . . .*'

He looked at the ceiling, his lips moving silently.

'No, wait a minute. . . . *When on your looks I dwell, my eyesight flickers . . . A Voice I hear: She is your dear—Be bold, take off her knickers.*'

So sternly reproving was Miss Teatime's immediate 'Mister Grope! You will kindly remember to whom you are speaking!' that Grope jumped and knocked the side of his head against the carved case of a wall clock. He looked hurt, bewildered, and quite harmless. Miss Teatime felt sorry for having startled him.

'You must not bring discredit on that beautiful uniform, you know,' she said kindly.

Grope recovered a little. 'You like it?'

'Very much.'

Proudly, 'It was a retirement present.'

Miss Teatime glanced once more at her watch and stood up. She hoped that Mr Grope's amorous urge had subsided. It would not be dignified to take part in an obstacle race through all that furniture.

Mr Grope took off the big peaked hat with RIALTO embroidered upon it in gold. He scratched his head.

'About what you were asking,' he said. 'I've had a thought.'

Not another erotic rhyme, prayed Miss Teatime.

But Grope had lumbered from the room. She heard his boots on the stair. Taking her opportunity, she slipped out into the corridor and stood close to the street door after making sure that it would open easily.

When he came downstairs again, he was holding something in his hand.

'I've been keeping one by,' he said. 'I meant to go to another doctor if Meadow didn't change his mind about stopping them. I'd have to have one to show, you see.'

He handed her a small brown-tinted bottle. On its label, headed AMIS & JEFFREY, CHEMISTS, EASTGATE, FLAXBOROUGH, was the instruction: "One to be taken, three times a day, after food."

Miss Teatime unscrewed the cap and tipped on to her palm the single table that the bottle contained. It was octagonal in shape and pale green. One face was stamped with the letters E.D.G.S.

'You can borrow it, if you like,' said Mr Grope. 'Promise to bring it back, though, won't you?'

'I shall, indeed. As soon as my department has identified this tablet—how pretty it is, by the way—and corrected its prescription records, I shall deliver it back to you personally. You have been most helpful, Mr Grope.'

She slid the octagon into the bottle. Grope leaned over her, watching the bottle disappear in her handbag.

'Marvellous pick-me-up, are those—They'd warm the blood of Eski-mos.'

Miss Teatime reached smartly for the latch and pulled open the door.

'If you happen not to be in when I return,' she said, 'I shall put it through the letter-box.'

'Until you come, my brain will burn—with thoughts of you without your frocks!'

Eluding the hand that sought to favour her posterior with a farewell squeeze, Miss Teatime hastened down the steps and made for her car.

She drove at once to Eastgate and parked as close as she could to the shop of Amis and Jeffrey. Before leaving the car, she transferred Mr Grope's tablet from its bottle to an envelope.

'I should like,' said Miss Teatime to one of two girls behind the counter, 'to speak to your chief dispenser, please.'

There appeared, after an interval of discussion at the back of the shop as to what so flattering a description as "chief dispenser" might portend, a wary-looking young man who said he was the manager and could he be of any assistance, Mrs, er . . . ?

'Miss,' she corrected sweetly. 'Yes, I have a small problem, but I am sure it can be resolved very quickly with your help.

'You see, an uncle of mine arrived last night to take a short holiday with me here in Flaxborough. He is a fairly elderly gentleman—quite spry, you understand, but getting on in years—and for some time he has been taking tablets prescribed by his doctor. Three every day, I believe. They probably are a simple tonic, but the Dean—my uncle, that is—does feel they are important to him.'

The manager, whose black, back-brushed hair and ebony-framed spectacles seemed to have been fashioned as a single headpiece to cap his sharp, sallow face, regarded her solemnly and without a trace of sympathy. Miss Teatime gave a little cough and persevered.

'He was most upset, as you may imagine, on discovering when he arrived that the box containing a week's supply of his tablets had burst during the journey. All but one of the tablets had shaken down and been lost through a hole in his pocket.

'Fortunately,'—she took the envelope from her handbag—'there was, as I say, this one survivor. You will see that it is distinctive in shape and colour. I should be most grateful if you could identify it so that my uncle may go to a doctor here in Flaxborough and obtain a repeat prescription.'

The manager was by now pouting very disagreeably. He glanced into the envelope, nodded, sniffed.

'Oh, yes. I know what that is.'

'Splendid!' she said. 'I was sure you would be able to help.'

'I said'—he handed back the envelope—'that *I* know what it is. I did not say that I could tell *you.*'

'Oh, but surely . . .'

'We are not allowed to divulge the names of drugs to members of the public. I'm sorry, madam. All I can suggest is that the gentleman consults a local doctor. Then, if the doctor cares to identify that tablet and to issue the appropriate prescription, we shall be pleased to dispense it.'

Miss Teatime had been looking at the manager's tie. It was fastened in the tightest, most diminutive knot she had ever seen.

'You'll appreciate that we cannot break the rules,' she heard him add. *(Unctuous sod, you'd not break wind if you thought it might oblige somebody.)*

'Naturally not. I shall tell the Dean what you advise.' She turned, paused, faced him again. 'Oh, by the way . . .' She was looking her most demure.

'Yes, madam?'

'You will think this unforgivably inquisitive of me,

but I do have a reason for asking. Tell me, in what year were you born?'

The irrelevance, the sheer impertinence of the question startled him so much that he answered it at once and without thinking.

'Nineteen thirty-six.' Then he scowled. 'Why?'

Miss Teatime looked him up and down appraisingly.

'Nineteen thirty-six . . . ah, yes. Quite a year for unsuccessful abortions, they tell me.'

CHAPTER TWELVE

Dr Meadow's surgery was a compact, single-storeyed building at the end of a short path leading off from the main drive to his house. It had been a carriage-house and stables in the earlier days of his father's practice. Where once had stood old Dr Ambrose Meadow's high-wheeled gig, there was now a three-litre Lagonda. The rest of the building had been reconstructed to form two consulting rooms, a small dispensary and receptionist's office, and a waiting-room with doors to the other three.

Miss Teatime arrived in the waiting-room a few minutes before six o'clock, which a printed notice on the wall proclaimed to be the time of evening surgery.

In her handbag was Mr Grope's green octagon.

In her head, daintily inclined in greeting to the group of people who were already assembled, was a story about the mislaying of a prescription provided by her London specialist and her hope that Dr Meadow would be able to identify the last of her present supply of tablets and give her a fresh order.

Miss Teatime, beckoned by a pretty, auburn-haired girl in a white coat, who had appeared at the hatch of her small office, gave her name and a London address.

'Are you a new patient?' the receptionist asked.

'You could say that I am a visitor. I have not yet chosen a regular doctor in Flaxborough.'

'Do you want to see Dr Bruce or Dr Meadow?'

'Oh, Dr Meadow, I think. He is the senior partner?'

'That's right.' The girl slipped the sheet of paper on which she had written Miss Teatime's name and address beneath a pile of three or four cards.

Miss Teatime took a seat and began unobtrusively to observe her fellow patients and to speculate upon their ills. They, equally unobtrusively, did the same to her.

A buzzer sounded weakly and a little glass panel above one of the doors flickered red.

The receptionist glanced at her top card.

'Mr Leadbetter.'

She handed the card to a florid, thick-set man who had risen to his feet with an air of grim determination. He stomped to the consulting room door and shut it firmly behind him.

A man with a grievance, Miss Teatime diagnosed.

She listened. So did everyone else. All that reached them of Mr Leadbetter's complaint was a prolonged muffled boom. Then came the gentle rise and fall of a sweetly reasoned remonstration by the golden-voiced Dr Meadow. More booming followed, but at a much reduced level and for a shorter time. Again the doctor's persuasive lilt. A pause. The lilt once more, livelier this time and crested with amusement. The boom—now friendly, responsive to the joke. An outside door clicked shut. Silence.

Smooth, thought Miss Teatime. Very smooth. Perhaps she should have asked to see Dr Bruce instead.

When the consumptive buzzer sounded again, the receptionist had to call 'Mrs Grope, please!' twice before there was any reaction from the stumpy, sad-looking woman with very dark eyes who sat opposite Miss Teatime. At the second, louder, summons, Mrs Grope jumped, looked round inquiringly at everybody in turn, then hurried to the wrong door. A woman with a thickly bandaged foot caught her sleeve and motioned her to the other.

So that, Miss Teatime reflected, was the partner of the poet of Blackfriars' Court. No wonder she had an air of chronic bewilderment.

Dr Bruce's sign was the next to light up. The bandaged woman hobbled into his consulting room. He disposed of her and three more patients before the senior partner's buzzer signified that he was no longer occupied with the woes of Mrs Grope.

'Mrs McCreavy. Will you go in now, please.'

Miss Teatime sneaked a look at Mrs McCreavy from behind an elderly copy of the *New Yorker* that she had been surprised to discover among the magazines on the table beside her. She saw a woman of about fifty, plump in black silk and tottery on too-tight shoes, who had the pained, querulous expression conferred by stubborn addiction to youthful make-up.

Mrs McCreavy paused at the door of Dr Meadow's room, tightened her scarlet bird-mouth into a secret smile, and squeezed through the doorway out of sight, as if to a scandalous assignation.

Dr Bruce continued his brisk dispatch of the ailing. His buzzer sounded five times in as many minutes. The waiting room had begun to look depopulated. Between calls, a typewriter clattered in the receptionist's office. She doubled as secretary, apparently.

Somewhere a clock struck the half hour. The girl left her typing in order to lock the surgery entrance against late arrivals. She smiled at Miss Teatime as she passed and gave a little shrug of mock weariness.

A schoolboy with his arm in a sling and a look of Napoleonic fortitude was next to disappear. There remained only Miss Teatime, a middle-aged man in a smart grey suit, and a girl of about twenty who kept her arms tightly folded across her chest and studied her shoes for most of the time.

Miss Teatime suppressed a yawn. She wondered what encyclopaedic symptoms lay beneath Mrs McCreavy's black silk. Ten minutes. Quarter of an hour. The man had had time to examine her intestines inch by inch and get them all back again by now.

'Excuse me . . .'

She started.

'Excuse me, but if you like . . .'

It was the gentleman in the grey suit, and he was leaning forward, talking to her.

'If you like, you can go in and see the doctor before I do. I am in no hurry.'

'That is remarkably kind of you.'

'Not at all. As a matter of fact, I am not a patient.'

Miss Teatime was tempted to say, Nor am I, but she turned it to 'No, I must say you look far too healthy to be consulting doctors.'

And so he did. His rather square face had the long-established tan of the widely travelled. It was a calm, controlled face, with a hint in the jaw muscles of considerable strength. His small moustache—military, Miss Teatime dubbed it, instinctively—was impeccably trimmed and almost white. The eyes, which she decided with regret to be humourless, were of very pale blue; they looked as if they had never been closed since early childhood.

The man had on the seat beside him a capacious

brief case of heavy leather, highly polished. Its flap was unlocked and the man had taken from it a sheaf of papers, which he held now on his knee. They looked like brochures or leaflets of some kind.

Ah, a salesman, Miss Teatime told herself. One thing about these pharmaceutical people, though—they had an air of distinction, of being concerned with higher things than mere money, that you never found in a groceries rep or a hawker of hardware.

She tried to confirm her guess by reading the bigger type on the topmost leaflet, but she was hampered by its being upside-down. Only one word could she make out without going nearer and putting on her glasses (and she could imagine no pretext for anything so brash as that). It was ELIXON. Not much help. She withdrew again behind her *New Yorker*.

A buzz proclaimed that Dr Bruce was free once more, but no one made a move. After a while, his consulting-room door opened and there appeared a tall, slightly bewildered looking man of about thirty-five, with thin, untidy hair and long hands that kept wrestling with each other. He gazed challengingly at the three people who were still waiting, shrugged, and went back into his room. Miss Teatime heard water begin to run. Dr Bruce doubtless was washing his hands of them all.

'Oh, by the way, Mr Brennan . . .'

The receptionist was leaning out of her hatch. The man in the grey suit looked up.

'Did you manage to see the doctor earlier on?' she asked him.

'No, I didn't, actually. There's no hurry. I shall wait now until he has finished surgery.'

There was some quality in his voice that Miss Teatime had detected before without being able quite to define it. Now she knew what it was: a slight lisp—not an affectation, but the kind of speech flaw that could have resulted from an injury.

'I just wondered,' the girl went on, 'because there was something I think he wanted to show you. It's a copy of that article he rang you about yesterday, and I've only just finished typing it.'

'That's fine. I'll take it with me when I go in, shall I? . . .' He put aside the leaflets and stood up.

The girl left the hatch and reappeared holding a long buff-coloured envelope which she handed to Brennan. He slipped it into an inside pocket and resumed his seat after thanking her and taking a casual glimpse of the desk where she had been typing.

For lack of anything else to do, Miss Teatime turned her attention to the girl with the folded arms. Why was she hugging herself like that, as if trying not to be noticed? She looked lonely and in trouble. Miss Teatime felt increasingly sorry for her. Some plausible Flaxborough buck had fed her one of the usual legends, no doubt. *It'll be all right if you run about a bit afterwards and drink plenty of water.* How sad that people were so ready to believe what they wanted to believe—or what others wanted them to bel . . .

There burst in upon this melancholy reflection a quick succession of violent sounds. A collision, as if of furniture . . . the crash of something overtoppled . . . a crumpling thud. Then, after an absolute silence no less shocking than the noise that had preceded it, the door to which all eyes turned seemed visibly to be straining against the assault upon it from within by a long, rasping scream.

For an absurdly extended time, nobody did anything. Did not convention decree that the right to intrude upon a doctor's privacy was strictly reserved to nurses or other doctors?

The dilemma was resolved when the door was suddenly dragged open by a Mrs McCreavy transformed by near-nudity and shock.

Clutching a bundle of snatched-up clothing to her breast, she staggered out of the room with head thrust forward and mouth open. Pert no longer, the brilliantly red lips looked like the edges of a deep, rawly inflicted cut which had drained her face of what little colour it had had.

The girl opposite Miss Teatime was the first to move. She sprang to Mrs McCreavy, put an arm round her shoulder, and led her to a chair.

Brennan stared at them, momentarily bewildered, then strode to the open door. Miss Teatime followed close behind.

On the floor of the consulting room lay Dr Meadow, face down. His arms and legs were disposed like those of a swimmer who had reached shore at last gasp and fallen at once to sleep. Near his head, and caught in a leg of the heavy office chair whose overturning they had heard, were the black coils of his stethoscope.

Brennan knelt. Miss Teatime watched the fine grey cloth of his jacket tighten against underlying muscle as he heaved Dr Meadow over and bent to listen to his chest.

Behind them, the receptionist had opened a window and was shouting 'Doctor Bruce!' Having found his room empty, she had looked out to see him getting into his car, which he had parked behind Meadow's big Lagonda.

'I think,' Brennan said, 'that the poor chap is dead.'

He raised his head and looked over his shoulder at Miss Teatime.

'Perhaps you had better try and find Dr Bruce.'

'The girl has been calling for him.' She listened. 'I believe I can hear someone coming in from outside now.'

Brennan turned again to the body. He felt one wrist, then the chest. He shook his head and got up slowly, buttoning his jacket. 'Extraordinary,' he murmured.

Bruce came into the room, pale-faced and anxious, yet quietly businesslike. Brennan and Miss Teatime moved aside to make way for him. They stood back close against the wall, silent spectators. From the doorway, the receptionist watched, knuckles pressed hard on her lower lip. The only sound was the muffled sobbing of Mrs McCreavy, who had been helped back into her crumpled dress and was now sitting grasping the hand of the girl with troubles.

Bruce squatted down beside his partner. Fingertips explored with delicate expertise. He unfastened Meadow's shirt, tugged his own stethoscope from his side pocket, and listened, head bowed.

After nearly half a minute, he took off his jacket, folded it several times, and beckoned the girl at the door.

'Slip it under his shoulders when I raise him. I want his head well back.'

The receptionist did as she was told.

'Ambulance,' Bruce said. He nodded towards the telephone on the desk. 'Then you'd better give the police a ring.'

The soft whirr of the spun dial sounded as loud as a helicopter rotor in the small, silent room.

Bruce crouched low, his mouth over Meadow's. Firmly, almost violently, he pressed the heel of his hand into the man's chest.

The girl was asking for an ambulance. She glanced

down at Dr Bruce and remembered something else. Would they please alert the resuscitation unit.

She dialled again.

The calm, matter-of-fact voice of the answering policeman made the scene around her seem suddenly unreal. She tried to give a simple account, but he sounded as if he wanted to sit there all day asking questions. She looked helplessly at Bruce. He interrupted what he was doing only long enough to inject a shot of adrenalin.

The voice at the other end became louder.

'I said, is he dead, Miss? Can you hear me?'

She started. 'Yes. Yes, I think he is.'

'You only *think . . . ?*'

She put down the phone.

When, at last, Bruce rose to his feet, he stared wearily at Meadow's body for several seconds before he stooped once more and gently eased free his folded jacket. He put it on and went out into the waiting-room. Brennan and Miss Teatime followed him.

The receptionist lingered unhappily by the consulting room door. She seemed to be wondering whether she ought to close it. Bruce touched her sleeve.

'Miss Sutton, would you mind staying on here until the ambulance comes. It shouldn't be many minutes. I must go round to the house now. Mrs Meadow will have to be told.'

Among the several matters exercising the busy mind of Miss Teatime was the reflection that her original purpose in visiting the surgery would not now be fulfilled. She watched the departure of the still tearful Mrs McCreavy in the custody of her younger companion, whose own anxiety, presumably, had been overlaid temporarily by the evening's excitement. What could Mrs McCreavy tell of Dr Meadow's dramatic end? She had volunteered not a single word and in the general distress no one had thought to ask her. The police, no doubt, would set that record straight in their own good time. Mr Brennan . . . had he gone yet? No, there he was by the door, his back towards her, putting the things back in his briefcase. A lost sale? Hardly. Those people were on a fairly easy pitch. Doctors did not like to think they were missing out on one of the latest fashions in miracle drugs. There had been a couple of those leaflets of his on the doctor's desk. ELIXON. Tall, dark blue letters. But what, for goodness' sake, was she to make of that other curious thing she had seen soon after entering Meadow's room? She would have to think about that. Most puzzling.

'Goodnight, Miss Sutton.'

Brennan was leaving. He nodded at Miss Teatime, then looked back to the girl.

'I'm very sorry.'

The door closed behind him.

Miss Teatime was about to follow, when she caught the expression of distressed appeal in the girl's eye. Of course—how thoughtless to leave her there alone. She went over to her and sat down. The girl looked at her gratefully.

After a while, the girl said: 'I hope it wasn't anything urgent you wanted to see the doctor about.'

'No, no,' Miss Teatime assured her. 'It was nothing that cannot wait a little longer.'

'I'm sure Dr Bruce would help if you like to stay until he comes back.'

'No, he has problems enough for one evening, poor man. I should not dream of troubling him with so trivial a matter. It was simply that I wished to obtain a repeat prescription for some tablets.'

stood patiently, with one hand resting on the back of a chair, apparently waiting for a break in the conversation between Bruce and the girl. A briefcase lay on the chair.

Miss Teatime had gone.

Bruce left the girl and came up to Purbright.

'What about Mrs Meadow?' Purbright asked him softly.

'At the hospital. She went in the ambulance.'

'Took their time a bit, didn't they?'

'Held up at the level crossing. Not that it would have made any difference.'

'He looked stone dead to me.'

'Oh, he was. No question about it.'

The whole of this exchange had been at a quiet, almost conspiratorial, level, with Bruce glancing occasionally at the man in grey. 'Wait a moment,' he now said to Purbright, 'I'll just see what that chap wants.'

He went across.

'Can I help you, Mr Brennan?'

Brennan made a small bow.

'I'm terribly sorry to make myself a nuisance at such a time, doctor, but there is something rather important which I should like to ask Miss Sutton.'

'Pauline,' Bruce called.

The girl joined them. Brennan seemed to be waiting for Bruce to leave, but the doctor made no move.

'It's this sentence,' Brennan said at last.

He unfolded the sheet of paper he had been hiding and pointed to a line near the top.

'I cannot quite understand it. Could you possibly have made an error in copying, do you think?'

The girl read, frowning.

'No, I . . . I don't think so, Mr Brennan.'

'Perhaps if we compared it with the original . . . ?'

'But I'm afraid you can't. Not now.'

Brennan raised his brows.

'Well, it's with the other things for posting that I took across to the house a few minutes ago just before Mrs Meadow left for the hospital.' She turned to Bruce. 'I thought that in the circumstances she ought to decide which letters should be sent off.'

'Quite right, Pauline.'

Brennan shrugged and gave a faint smile.

'I suppose,' Bruce said doubtfully, 'that you could call later and explain to Mrs Meadow . . .'

'No, I would not dream of it. The matter is of no consequence.'

Brennan slipped the sheet of typescript into his case, gave another short bow, turned and left.

Bruce apologized to Purbright for the interruption.

'Miss Sutton tells me that you'd like to put a few questions to her, inspector. Perhaps you could do that first. It's been a rather trying day for her.'

'Of course. Now then, Pauline, what I am going to have to do is make a report to the coroner. That is standard procedure in all cases of sudden death. It doesn't mean that we are suspicious of anybody. We just have to establish exactly what happened.'

He searched in his pockets until he had found an envelope and a short piece of pencil.

'Firstly, I should like to know when you yourself last saw Dr Meadow.'

'About half-past four this afternoon.'

'As long ago as that?'

'Yes, I'd been typing an article for him. That and a few letters. He went back to the house at half-past four to get his tea.'

'What about your tea?'

'I made a cup here. He didn't tell me until I'd finished typing his article that he wanted a copy made, so I stayed on.'

'At what time did surgery begin?"

'Six o'clock.'

'And didn't you see him then?'

'No, he always came into his consulting room by its own side door and rang for the first patient when he was ready.'

'I see. He seemed fit, did he, when he left you at four-thirty?'

'Perfectly. I've never known him to be anything else, as a matter of fact.'

'Perhaps I should say,' interjected Dr Bruce, 'that my parnter was, in fact, suffering a certain degree of hypertension. Miss Sutton here wouldn't have known that, of course, but I think you'll find that Dr James, in Priorgate, will confirm what I say.'

'Dr James was treating him, was he?'

'Well, he was certainly advising him. That I do know.'

Purbright again faced the receptionist.

'I presume that someone was with Dr Meadow when he collapsed. A patient.'

'Yes. Mrs McCreavy. She's been taken home.'

'I'll have her address, if I may.'

The girl went to the hatch and returned with the bunch of record cards. Purbright looked at them.

'Are these all patients who were seen by Dr Meadow this evening?'

'Not all. These three. Mr Leadbetter was first in. Then Mrs Grope . . .'

'Mrs Grope? Mr Walter Grope's wife?'

'That's right. And Mrs McCreavy was the last. A girl called Hewson was waiting and so was the lady you met when you came in—Miss . . . Teatime, is it?'

'Miss Teatime,' the inspector confirmed ruminatively. 'Miss Lucilla Edith Cavell Teatime.'

He wrote down the names and addresses of Mrs McCreavy and Leadbetter.

'Oh, and I'd better have yours, Pauline, while I'm at it.'

She told him.

'What was Mrs McCreavy's reaction, by the way?'

'Oh, she screamed blue murder and came rushing out with half her clothes off.' The girl seemed to repent of the note of contempt in her voice; she added quickly, 'Well, it must have given her a nasty fright, I expect.'

'Did you go in to see what had happened?'

'No, I ran to try and find Dr Bruce. It was Mr Brennan who went into Dr Meadow's room. Him and Miss Teatime.'

'Mr Brennan is the gentleman who was here a little while ago?'

'That's right.'

'But he's not a patient, I gather.'

Bruce shook his head. 'He's the new rep for Elixon. One of the drug houses.'

'Where should I be able to get in touch with him? If it proves necessary—I don't say that it will.'

Bruce looked blank, but the girl replied: 'The Elixon man stays at the Roebuck as a rule, I believe. They'd tell you how long he's booked in for.'

'But might it not be just overnight?'

'Oh, no. Reps are usually here for at least a week. They work the whole area from Flax and then go on to Norwich or over to Leicester. I should think Mr Brennan will be around for another three or four days.'

'I see. Well, you might as well get along home now, Pauline. Thank you for being so helpful.'

When the girl had gone, Purbright turned to meet the speculative eye of Dr Bruce. For a while he said nothing. Then he smiled.

'Yes?' Bruce prompted.

The inspector produced cigarettes. He lit one after Bruce had waved back the proffered packet.

'You are thinking,' said Purbright, 'this . . . Why has an inspector, of all people, trotted along here so promptly on hearing of the regrettable, but perfectly natural, collapse and death of a respected general practitioner? Am I right?'

'You are,' said Bruce, drily.

'Ah, well you must not read too much into my apparent enthusiasm. For one thing, Sergeant Malley—whose province this sort of thing is—had gone home to enjoy a well-earned meal and it seemed rather heartless to drag him back again.'

'That was not your only reason.'

'No, it wasn't. I admit to a degree of personal curiosity. You see, there's a strong element of coincidence. You probably are not aware of it, doctor.'

'I am not.'

'Let me explain. Some rather odd things have been going on in Flaxborough lately. As you must know, if only by reading the local paper, a number of women have been assaulted. I don't need to go into details, but the nature and the unusual frequency of these attacks have suggested that the persons responsible—and I use the plural advisedly—constitute a medical rather than a criminal problem.

'One of them, and only one, is known. Unfortunately, he is now dead . . .'

'Old Winge, you mean?'

'Yes. Alderman Winge. As I say, he is dead. But he was a patient of your late partner. Coincidence? All right. Now then, a girl was attacked just outside this surgery—out there on Heston Lane. Who came to her rescue? Dr Meadow, as you probably have heard. And there is no doubt in my mind but that he saw and recognized the man responsible—whom he let go, incidentally.

'Again, observation is being kept at this moment on a man whose wife is convinced that he goes out at night to seek some sort of erotic satisfaction. I know this sounds questionable as evidence, but I do happen to know that this particular man showed no such tendencies until recently, when he moved to Flaxborough and became a patient of Dr Meadow.

'You may say that these links, if I might call them that, are few and extremely tenuous. But I'm sure you will understand my curiosity—to put it no higher—on hearing that the man I believed to know a lot more than he had divulged about the business had suddenly dropped dead.'

For a long time, Dr Bruce gazed mournfully out of the window. When he spoke, it was with slow, rather weary deliberation.

'Whatever you say now, inspector, is scarcely likely to remove the implication you've already succeeded in making.'

'Which is?'

'That my partner's death was connected in some way with what you've been talking about. That it wasn't natural, in other words.'

'I'm a long way from saying that, doctor. I am not even going to speculate at this stage. After all, the cause of death has not been established. When it is—and I don't suppose there'll be any difficulty there—I shall accept the findings of the experts, as will the coroner. In the meantime, though, coincidence does exist. Judgment must be suspended, but investigation must not. Hence'—the inspector smiled—'the snooping. You do understand?'

Bruce resignedly lifted and let fall his hand.

'Very well. Is there anything you want to ask me now? I don't want to be much longer getting over to the hospital, and I've some home visits I shall have to fit in.'

'I'll be as brief as I can. Firstly, the cause of death. Do you want to say what you think it was?'

'Oh, a coronary. I don't think there can be any doubt about that. He died extremely quickly, you know.'

'Obviously you wouldn't have had time to make a detailed examination, but did you notice anything—anything at all—that seemed odd at the time, or has since struck you as being odd?'

Bruce pondered.

'Not a thing. The whole scene was exactly as one would have expected. He must have blacked out and gone full length.'

'But wouldn't he have been sitting in his chair? Doctors never seem to get up when they're being consulted by me.'

Bruce's manner eased a fraction. 'Perhaps you consult them about the wrong things. No, I imagine my partner was standing up in order to examine the McCreavy woman's chest. She was half undressed when she ran out, you know.'

'According to Miss Sutton, he saw only three patients this evening. Yet she had quite a pile of cards. You must have dealt with far more than three in the same period.'

'Yes, that was the usual pattern.'

'You mean he was—what?—more leisurely in his dealings with patients?'

'If you like. Look—I'm the junior partner, he was the senior. Every practice works on the sound old principle that the junior's share of the work shall equal the senior's share of the income. What could be fairer?'

'What, indeed.' Purbright walked to the door and threw out the end of his cigarette. 'In that case, I assume Dr Meadow tended to be selective. Did he deal primarily with those we might call his regulars?'

'Naturally.'

'Could you list them? In categories, I mean, not as individuals.'

'No difficulty about that. The paying patients. The socially desirable. And a few of the interestingly elderly.'

'Ah,' said Purbright, 'it's the old ones that I've been finding interesting lately. When I retire from the police force, perhaps I'll take up geriatrics. Incidentally . . .'

Bruce watched Purbright search through a collection of pieces of paper he had taken from his pocket, select one, and thrust the rest back.

'Do you happen to know,' the inspector asked, 'anything about a substance called'—he frowned at his note—'beta-aminotetrylglutarimide, God forgive us?'

'Where on earth did you get that one from?'

'It was mentioned during the inquest on Winge. I can't vouch for my pronunciation. Nor for lawyer Scorpe's.'

'Scorpe—he asked about it, did he?'

'Yes. He put it to Meadow.'

After a pause, Bruce said: 'No, I don't know what it is, but I suppose the old man's family must have nosed around and found that Meadow had been prescribing it for Winge.'

'That was my impression.'

'I know those vultures. I smell a lawsuit.'

'So did Meadow, I think. He dragged in a red herring right away. He told Scorpe that Winge had been going against his advice and dosing himself with a herbal remedy called Samson's Salad. You haven't heard of *that,* I suppose?'

'Good God, no. What's it supposed to do?'

'Impart the sexual virility of the Ancient Britons.'

Bruce took a little time to digest this promising specification. Then he said, half in wonder, half in pride:

'We don't half have some goings-on in this little old town.'

'Don't we?'

The inspector stood and buttoned his raincoat. At the door, he raised his hand.

'Ring me if you get any ideas.'

CHAPTER FOURTEEN

Miss Teatime paused at the little Georgian doorway that led to her rooms in the Church Close, and, while feeling for her key, looked up at the gothic wedding cake tiers of the great tower of St Laurence's. That miraculous stone confection never failed to please her. She loved in particular its ever-changing response to weather and time of day. In the first light of morning, its buttresses, lancets and galleries had a metallic sharpness; they looked to be fashioned in pewter. Then, as the sky brightened, silver facets appeared. Summer noons turned the traceries to honeycomb. In storm, the tower was a monochrome of granite; in mist, a long brown sail, becalmed. As Miss Teatime gazed at it now, an hour after sunset on a damp, still evening, the soaring stone was tinged with green, as if it had caught and thrown down to her a reflection of the fields and woods beyond the town.

She sighed and faced about to open the door.

In her sitting-room at the head of the first flight of narrow, sharply twisting stairs, she switched on the light and enjoyed for a moment its revelation of pale lavender colour-washed walls and the gleam of fresh grey paint from deep, classically simple window frames. She had decorated the room herself, transforming it from the dinginess of long neglect (which had made it a gratifying cheap buy) into what she imagined—probably rightly—would have pleased those Flaxborough contemporaries of Jane Austen who had been its first occupants.

She took off her hat and coat, made tea in the tiny adjoining kitchen, and drew up a chair to the slender-legged table beneath one of the wall lamps. Among the contents of the tea tray, which she had set down at the end of the table away from typewriter and stationery, was a small whiskey bottle, half full.

When she judged the tea to be properly infused, she poured some out and added a little sugar, a very little milk, and as much whiskey as would still allow the mixture to be stirred without slopping over into the saucer. She took a sip, then, with an increasing approval, another, and a third. She did not care for over-hot tea: blowing it was vulgar—it also wastefully evaporated the whiskey.

Not until she had finished her first cup and poured and laced her second, did Miss Teatime turn her attention to a clip of correspondence which she had laid ready beside the typewriter.

There were nearly a dozen letters, all addressed to Moldham Meres Laboratories. Although most were from individual customers, four had been written by the managers of health food stores in various parts of the country.

They related to Press reports of the Winge inquest. Some enclosed newspaper cuttings. *Drowned Alderman was Herb Eater . . . Reservoir Death after 'Salad', Court Told . . . Doctor Blames Nature Cure.*

Every writer declared, in terms ranging from the abrupt and offensive to the politically ingenious (a customer in Leamington Spa suggesting that Samson's

Salad was a paralysing nerve weed cultivated on Siberian state farms), that no further supplies were required. Some of the shopkeepers demanded a refund on current stocks.

It was this last category of complaint that Miss Teatime considered particularly wounding, indicative as it was of a degree of cupidity that she had scarcely expected to find in the protagonists of Natural Goodness.

She lit a cheroot and considered how best a reply could be framed. It would have to be in the nature of a duplicated circular, she feared: these letters were doubtless but harbingers of flocks to come.

After a while, she began to type. Her typing, though punctuated by periods of thought, had the grace, speed and accuracy typical of an old and hard school of secretarial training. Ah, yes, the Bishop (she would have explained to an admiring onlooker) had always insisted upon his pastoral letters being absolutely clean.

> Friend, (her manifesto ran)
>
> I am extremely sorry that you have been disturbed by certain newspaper references to Our Product. Our legal advisers, needless to say, are already taking certain action, in the outcome of which we have complete confidence; but I am writing to you in the meantime to point out certain facts which you, as an intelligent person, are fully entitled to interpret for yourself.
>
> Firstly, I must reveal to you that the medical practitioner who saw fit to make the disparaging remarks in question has since died suddenly. We do not, of course, claim this un-unfortunate occurrence to have been divinely engineered in vindication of Nature's Way. You might well wonder, however, whether a man so signally unsuccessful

in maintaining his own life span was qualified to throw doubt upon the health-winning methods of others.

Secondly, I would point out that Moldham Meres Laboratories have never pretended that Our Product is incapable of being misused. There is no Gift of Nature which cannot be turned to a wrongful purpose. Our Product is a natural concentrate of the Life Force. Therefore it cannot fail to increase the Vitality of the user and thus greatly to improve the performance of all Natural Functions.

You will readily appreciate, of course, that only those who temper their enjoyment of life with Self Control and respect the confines of Matrimony are suitable candidates for the advantages offered by Our Product.

If, for any reason, you feel that your own Personal Standards do not meet this condition, we shall be happy to refund your money on receipt of Proof of Purchase.

Miss Teatime withdrew the sheet from the machine and carefully read it through. From time to time she nodded to herself. Plenty of capital letters. Excellent. Devotion to upper case, she had noticed, was one of the more consistent characteristics of Life Force enthusiasts.

She put the letter aside. She would make the stencil later, then Florrie could start running off some copies.

It was now quite dark outside in the Close. There stood out from the blackness opposite an arched multicoloured glow. It was the stained glass window of the chapel where choir practice was usually held. Miss Teatime gazed fondly at the night-framed mosaic of indigo, ruby and saffron. How timelessly dependable it looked, this lovely survival of mediaeval self-confidence.

She refilled her cup and carried it to a small chintz-covered armchair near the fireplace. Close to the chair was a telephone on a low table. She set down her cup, lowered herself into the chair and reached for the phone. She asked for a Welbeck number and waited, leaning back into the comfort of the cushions.

'Bernard? . . . This is Lucilla—Lucilla Teatime.'

'Lucy! My dear, how lovely to hear you again! Where are you?'

She smiled smugly to herself and stroked with one finger the outline of a flower in the patterned chair cover.

'I am a long way from London, and not a bit sorry. Flaxborough suits me admirably.'

'Where and what in God's name is Flaxborough?'

'Now, Bernard,' she said reprovingly, 'I thought better of you. To pretend that civilization stops at North-west Three is the least endearing of the Londoner's parochial affectations. Flaxborough is not merely an exceptionally charming town; it is a good deal more stimulating than that elephantine combination of a clip joint and knocking shop that you are pleased to regard as the centre of the universe.'

'All right, Lucy, all right. Just tell me what you are doing.'

'A number of things. All interesting.'

'And rewarding? Your talents are sadly missed, my love.'

'I really believe you mean that. But you need not worry. This is a town of many opportunities.'

'Which you are in the process of seizing, no doubt.'

'I glean where I may, Bernard. With a little help, of course.'

'Oh?'

'At the moment—and I know you will be interested to hear this—it is being given by an old friend of yours. You did not know, did you, that Brother Culpepper is here with me?'

'Good Lord! Holy Joe?'

'You had not heard that he was in retreat?'

'Well, I did gather as much from the newspapers.'

'No, no, Bernard—I mean in an ecclesiastical sense. Out here he is isolated from the demands of the world. He tells me it is a great relief not to feel sought after all the time. And of course the open air life is working wonders for him.'

'Never mind Joe. I want to hear about you, Lucy. What are you doing with yourself?'

'I have acquired a herb farm.'

'A *what?*'

'A herb farm. Now, please do not interrupt, Bernard: this call is going to cost rather a lot of money, and you will have to listen carefully if you are to understand what I wish you to do for me. There is one thing I must be clear about before I begin. Am I right in assuming that your—what shall I say?—your professional lustre is undimmed?'

There was a slight pause.

'If you mean what I think you mean, the answer is yes.'

'Oh, I am so glad. In that case, I am sure you will be able to do me the favour I have in mind. It will require a little research—nothing terribly difficult. Now then, Bernard, are you ready? You will probably wish to make a note or two.'

'Carry on.'

'Firstly, I wish to know what you can find out about a Dr Augustus Meadow, who is in practice in Heston Lane, Flaxborough. Or was, rather—he happened to die this evening.'

'Oh, Lucy, you surely haven't got yourself mixed up in . . .'

'Certainly not. As far as anybody knows, he collapsed and died in a perfectly respectable manner and in his own surgery. It was by sheer coincidence that I was waiting to see him at the time. The annoying thing is that I shall not now be able to learn from him what I wanted.'

'What sort of information are you after, anyway? Career? Background? Whatever I can unearth down here is bound to be pretty sketchy. Why don't you see what you can find in the files of the local paper? I assume there *is* a local paper?'

'I am not writing a biography, Bernard. My interest is in the man's professional activities and I have reason to think that some of them may have been specialized in a way that would gain notice. His receptionist tells me that he conducted certain clinical trials, or helped to conduct them, on behalf of a drug firm called Elixon. According to her, he published findings in the medical press. I suggest that back numbers of the *British Medical Journal* might be revealing. Unfortunately, that is not the sort of literature one finds knocking about in Flaxborough public library, or I might not be troubling you.'

'All right, I'll cast around. Anything else?'

'Yes. Have you heard of a drug called "Juniform"?'

'I have.'

'Is it well known?'

'Not in my field, no. But then it's scarcely likely to become part of the armoury of the obstetrician.'

'Oh, Bernard! You are sweet. Obstetrician. . . . So you are!'

'Now look, Lucy—do you want me to help you or don't you?'

At once Miss Teatime quelled her trill of amusement. 'Bernard, I *am* sorry. No, you were saying . . . ?'

'I was saying—or about to say—that "Juniform" is what you might call an over-sixties drug. I've no personal experience of it, but I do know that it is being very assiduously pushed.'

'But how exciting! Like heroin, you mean?'

'No, I do not mean like heroin. Pushed commercially. It isn't a pep pill being peddled round coffee bars. Private surgeries are where the pressure is being applied. The manufacturers obviously think they've got a winner. I gather they're spending like mad on promotion.'

'I see. . . . And what exactly is "Juniform" supposed to accomplish?'

'The claim, I gather, is that it produces some kind of cellular modification that inhibits natural ageing processes. Is that too technical for you?'

'Hence the name, I presume. "Juniform." *Juvenis*, young.'

'Exactly. I'll try and dig up some more about it, if you really want me to.'

'I do, my dear. It sounds enormously intriguing.'

'At least I know your interest is purely altruistic, Lucy. It will be a good many years before *you* need any artificial rejuvenation.'

'Bernard, you are quite irresistible! No wonder all those lovely rich women bring you their cysts to be . . .'

'Is there,' he interrupted hastily, 'anything else you want me to find out while I'm at it?'

'Am I being a dreadful nuisance?'

'Not in the least. I'm only too happy to help.'

'Well, in that case, I shall be greedy and ask you for one final piece of information. This will not be easy, I am afraid, but I know you will try. It concerns Elixon —you know, the drug house that markets "Juniform". I wish to know whatever you can learn about one of its travelling representatives. His name is Brennan, and he is at present in this area. Oh, and Bernard . . .'

'Yes?'

'I realize that this will sound quite wickedly unreasonable, but if all this information is going to be of any use to me, I must have it within twenty-four or, at the most, forty-eight hours.'

'Bloody hell!'

'Bloody hell, indeed, Bernard, but I did tell you that Flaxborough is a considerably more lively town than London. I think the absence of petrol fumes has something to do with it. You will ring me?'

'Oh, all right. But I'm not promising anything.'

'Flaxborough four-three-double-seven. Tomorrow evening, or the evening following at the very latest.'

'I'll see what I can do.'

'Which I know will be a great deal, my dear. You are a man of resource. My confidence will not miscarry . . .'

'Lucy! For God's sake! Not over the phone. . . .'

'Sorry,' she said sweetly.

But the line was already dead.

CHAPTER FIFTEEN

Mrs McCreavy greeted Inspector Purbright with a mixture of apprehension and curiosity. She had never, in the course of a somewhat tediously blameless life, received a visit from a policeman of any rank, let alone a detective inspector. But now, with so elevated a representative of the law upon her doorstep, it seemed (to Mrs McCreavy) that neglectful destiny was going to make up for lost time. Into what sort of notoriety was she about to be plunged? Would there be a taking of photographs? A summons to court? And had she remembered, on hearing the door bell, to take that corset off the settee in the front room?

She preceded him into the parlour, ready to whisk the corset under a cushion. It was nowhere in sight. (Of course—she'd put it away earlier that morning when the window cleaner had called.) Feeling less vulnerable, she tightened up her face and invited him to state his business.

'I understand, Mrs McCreavy, that you were present in Dr Meadow's surgery yesterday evening when he was taken ill.'

She bowed her head in solemn confirmation.

'It must have been a very upsetting experience for you. I'm sorry.'

'Upsetting,' she repeated. 'Yes, definitely.'

'I hope you're feeling a little better now.'

'A little. Thank you very much.'

'The reason I am here is quite simple, Mrs McCreavy. You have nothing to worry about. It is just that a sudden death of this kind has to be officially reported. We have to establish details. You understand? All quite usual.'

'Details. I see.'

'So I want you to tell me exactly what happened, as you remember it. Of course, I shan't ask you anything private—about your reasons for consulting Dr Meadow, I mean. I only want you to describe what took place.'

Mrs McCreavy's response suggested that the inspector's delicacy had been wasted. She slid both hands across her diaphragm and lifted, as if for his approbation, a generously proportioned bosom.

'Well, I'd been getting these pains round here, you see. Oh, and right through the chest. Just like knives. A bit worse on this side, if anything.'

She thoughtfully weighed her left breast, reminding Purbright, despite his determination to be seriously sympathetic, of a judge at a vegetable show.

'Of course, I've had them, off and on, since I was a girl, and my husband always says I make a lot of fuss about nothing, but I mean, he doesn't know, does he? He's not in there to feel. And then there was Mrs Holland, next door but one. She had to have all her insides taken away. Well . . .' She paused, inviting comment.

'You were very wise to make sure,' Purbright said briskly. 'So,' he continued at once, 'you went to the surgery, entered Dr Meadow's consulting room when it was your turn, and told him about the pains. He was sitting down, was he?'

'Yes,' Mrs McCreavy seemed a little resentful at having been short-circuited.

'How did his appearance strike you? Did he look ill or tired?"

'No, nothing like that. He seemed a bit quiet, though, and he didn't listen properly at first when I was talking to him. He just sat fiddling with that thing they listen to your heart through.'

'Anyway, you told him your symptoms, I suppose. What happened then?'

'He told me to take my things off.'

'Yes.'

'Well, I did. Not altogether, I mean. Just . . . well, so that he could sound my chest. There's a screen, of course. When I came out again, he was standing up. He got me to come around beside the desk. Next to him—you know, facing. Anyway, he started off by doing that tapping business with two fingers, up and down the chest, and then round the back. I always like that, don't you? He'd got lovely hands, Dr Meadow had. They sort of matched his voice—do you know what I mean? Anyway, he went on tapping and asking questions for a bit, about where I felt the pain, and whether I'd had a cold, and what I ate, and that sort of thing, and then he put on his what's-its-name—you know—not telescope . . .'

'Stethoscope.'

'That's right—and he went over my chest again with that, and he said there was nothing wrong that he could hear, absolutely nothing. And then he got me to turn round and he started listening at the back. And he said, no, nothing there. Oh, he said that twice, and I thought he sounded a little bit annoyed, as a matter of fact.

And then he sort of stepped away. I didn't see him, of course, but I heard him say something like, "Well, we'll see if this does the trick", and I waited, and then I felt that thing go on my back again, and I heard him say something very quietly to himself. It sounded like, "The fur is darker" . . .'

'The fur is darker?'

'That's right. I don't know what he could have meant. The fur is darker—that's what he said. I only thought of it afterwards because of what happened. You see, straight away there was this funny hissing noise he made. Ssss! Like that. As if he was impatient or cross. And then I got the fright of my life. Well, his arm came up as if he was trying to grab me. And me with practically nothing on. I thought . . . well, I don't know what I thought, but I jumped away from him and I think I called out "Get away", or "Don't", or something, and then there was this awful crash and I looked round and there he was lying on the floor, sort of jerking and twitching, and I screamed and all I can remember after that was sitting out there in the waiting-room and crying and trying to drink a glass of water that Miss Sutton had brought me. Oh, it was a terrible shock to see him there. . . . Poor Dr Mea . . .'

A return of grief transformed the name into a soft, bleating sob. Her head fell. She felt ineffectually for the handbag that she had put down on the settee on coming in. It was just out of reach. Purbright stood and moved it over against her hand. He touched her shoulder.

'Thank you, Mrs McCreavy. I shan't trouble you any more.'

And he didn't. But as he walked down the path between the diminutive lawn and a bed of Mr McCreavy's scrupulously tended dahlias towards the green-painted gate, he reflected on troubles of his own. Not the least of these was the bafflement induced by the late Dr Meadow's last words.

What on earth had he been trying to convey by "The fur is darker?" What fur? Had there been an animal of some kind in the surgery? Had it bitten him? Fatally? Oh, hell. . . .

Sergeant Love was looking deceptively bland when Purbright got back to the police station.

'I see he's still at it,' he announced.

'Who's at what?' Purbright was in no mood for cryptic references.

'The Flaxborough Crab. Have you seen the report book this morning?'

'I have seen nothing this morning. I've been purging my soul by unproductive leg work.'

'Another young woman's been attacked.'

Purbright's weary 'Oh, Christ!' implied that he had had about enough of the conspiracy by assault-prone females to disrupt his routine. But at once he repented and asked anxiously: 'Serious?'

'She wasn't hurt. Only frightened. He was wearing something round his face this time.'

'That's new.'

'Yes.'

'Who's the girl?'

'Elizabeth Loder. Nineteen. She's a housemaid. Her family live in Dorley Road, but she's only there on her nights off. Anyway, it was Pook who interviewed her. He's doing you a full report.'

'Is he. Yes, all right, Sid. Now look—did you manage to see that Leadbetter character?'

'Aye, Mrs Grope, stoo. She says her old man's cooling off again. Very pleased about that. Apparently the doctor told her that Grope had been taking some medicine that might have disagreed with him but that he'd had it stopped.'

'She offered no clue about Meadow's dropping dead I suppose?'

'No, she said he was perfectly all right when she came out.'

'I see. And Leadbetter?'

Love grinned. 'Funny, but do you know who he is? He's the brother of that old ram on the council—the one who was mixed up in that brothel business a few years back. Must run in the family.'

'Must run in Dr Meadow's patients,' corrected Purbright, thoughtfully. 'Unless Leadbetter's another herb addict. Did he tell you what it was he'd gone to see the doctor about?'

'Not a word.'

'No, I hardly expected he would.'

It was very rarely that Love felt awkward in the inspector's presence. Purbright was no wielder of rank, and his temperament was remarkably equable. Today, however, not even the sergeant's cheery insensibility could long block his realization that Purbright was, in the sergeant's terminology, "bloody well cheesed". He ventured, crudely but with good intent, to find out why.

'Do you reckon old Meadow was knocked off?'

Purbright looked up. His expression was one of agreeable surprise, almost of gratitude.

'Ah, I knew if I waited long enough I wouldn't be left alone in that lunatic surmise. You've come to join me, have you, Sid?'

Guessing that he had fortuitously said the right thing, the sergeant gave a self-congratulatory grin and gazed at his feet.

'Come on and sit down, then. Let's see what we can make of it all. If anything.'

Purbright shifted his chair along a little and collected into a tidy group the reports and notes that lay on his desk.

'Tell you what,' he went on. 'You can be a stand-in for the Chief Constable. He's the one I ought to be talking to, but I've neither the heart nor the nerve at the moment. By the way, do you know where Bill Malley is?'

'He went over to the hospital about half an hour ago. I believe he's seeing the deputy coroner as well.'

'Good. That means they'll be getting on with the post-mortem. Everything is going to depend on that. We've nothing else. Not a damned thing. So if Heineman doesn't manage to turn anything up, we can all go home.'

'You said Dr Bruce thought it was a natural death. He did examine him, didn't he?'

'As far as he could in the circumstances. He was only giving an opinion. Incidentally, do you know anything about Bruce?'

'Not a lot. He hasn't been here very long.'

'How long?'

'About eighteen months, two years. They reckon he's a bit of a live wire. From what I hear, he's been doing all the donkey work.'

'I wonder,' said Purbright, ruminatively, 'if donkeys ever kick.'

'That's mules.'

The inspector shook his head.

'I don't know—the whole trouble is that the very idea of a respectable doctor being cunningly assassinated in his own surgery is so bloody far-fetched that one can't help being fascinated by it. The sensible thing is to reject it out of hand. Damn it all, there isn't any evidence. None at all. And yet that only makes the notion more attractive, somehow. You see now, don't you, why I don't dare discuss this with the chief? He'd think I'd blown a gasket.'

'He wouldn't be very sympathetic,' Love agreed.

While lighting a cigarette, Purbright glanced at one of the sheets before him.

'I wouldn't care so much,' he said, 'if only there were somebody who by any stretch of imagination qualified as a suspect. But just look at this miserable bloody list. They're the only people who were anywhere near the man at the time.

'Bruce, the overworked assistant partner. Disliked Meadow, certainly. He'd have had access to poisons and the knowledge to use one that would produce symptoms consistent with a fatal onset of Meadow's blood pressure trouble. What does he gain, though? Junior partners aren't heirs apparent; he doesn't automatically take over the practice. Anyway, there's the hell of a long gap between dislike, or even strong resentment, and the sort of hatred that makes people murder one another.'

'Perhaps,' Love suggested, 'he was after the old man's missus. Doctors are devils for that sort of caper.'

Purbright regarded him sternly for a moment. 'Have you met Mrs Meadow?'

The sergeant shrugged. 'It was just a thought.'

'There are oddities enough in this business, Sid, without your adding to them. However, now that you've mentioned the wife, I'm reminded that we know very little about the domestic background. Mrs Meadow can't be ruled out, strictly speaking, any more than Bruce can. She's part of the clutter, if you see what I mean. She had opportunity, probably knowledge and means. Temperament?—possibly. Motive?—we've no idea, and we're not likely to find out with her help.

'The receptionist, Pauline Sutton. Out. I think we're safe there, at any rate. Then there were three patients who actually consulted Meadow, also a youngish girl who came and went without seeing him, a traveller from some pharmaceutical firm who was waiting to see him but only went into his room when the doctor was either dead already or as near as dammit, and finally our venerable friend, Miss Teatime.'

'Yes, what was *she* after?' asked Love.

'She didn't confide in me, but I'd guess that she intended to tackle Meadow about his remarks at the Winge inquest. He hadn't exactly gone out of his way to boost the herb trade.'

'It's just as well for her,' Love said, 'that she didn't get in to see him *before* he kicked the bucket.'

'Decidedly. The same applies to the rep, for that matter—what's-his-name, Brennan.'

'Have you seen him since?'

'No, but I rang him last night at the Roebuck and told him he was likely to be called as a witness at the inquest. He promised to keep himself available.'

'When *is* the inquest, by the way?'

'That's what I'm waiting to hear now. I assume Malley will have fixed it with Thompson. Right, where were we?' Purbright looked again at his file.

'The patients,' Love reminded him.

'Yes, the three who actually went into the consulting room. The last three people to see Meadow alive. One private. Two National Health. Any significant distinction there, Sid, in regard to homicidal tendencies? One man, two women. There you are—what a chance for applied psychology. You've talked with Leadbetter. You've talked with mother Grope. I've talked with Mrs McCreavy, and I make you a present of the information that she'd have neither the guile nor the guts to kill a sick chicken. Right, then. You've got the facts. Spot the murderer. I pass.'

Love watched Purbright throw himself back in his chair and draw a final desperate mouthful of smoke from his cigarette before reaching out and angrily stubbing it in the ashtray.

'Of course, it could be,' Love ventured, with the air of advancing a novel and utterly comforting proposition, 'that Dr Meadow died of natural causes after all. I mean . . . well, I only asked about the other because you seemed worried.'

Purbright stared, opened his mouth and closed it again, scowled, then at last relaxed into a posture of weary acceptance.

'Yes, you're perfectly right. This is just so much pointless, time-wasting speculation. Sheer self-indulgence on my part. It comes to something when we start trying to catch a criminal before we know there's been a crime.'

'I expect you had a hunch,' suggested the sergeant, kindly. Hunches, his reading of fiction informed him, were perfectly permissible excuses for queer behaviour in the upper ranks.

'That's nothing but another name for pre-judging an issue,' Purbright retorted, ungratefully. 'The only sensible course now is to wait for the post-mortem report.'

'What happens if it's negative?'

'It won't be.'

Purbright suddenly slapped the desk with his hand.

'Look, Sid—we've been messed about for weeks by citizens with the staggers who attack women. We don't know how many, probably we never shall know. The only one we've nailed—or who nailed himself, rather —had been getting a certain drug from Meadow. Another man on the drug was known to be acting along similar lines, if not violently. But now, to use your phrase, he's cooled off. Harper confirms that, by the way. And why the change? Obvious. Meadow stopped the drug. Who was it who actually caught and must have recognized one of these Crab characters? Meadow. Why did he keep quiet? Again I think the reason's obvious. It was one of his own patients—and probably an influential one, at that. Leadbetter? He lives just off Heston Lane, near where the Sweeting girl was attacked. I know Perce Leadbetter. It's only by the grace of God and relatives that he hasn't got a record for indecent assault. I didn't tell you that when I asked you to see him, but I thought you knew. And it's a hundred to one that Perce's reason for turning up at Meadow's surgery last night was to ask for another supply of pep pills.'

'Pep pills?' Love clearly considered such things alien to respectable medical practice.

'Well, what else can they be? They certainly got old Winge's tail wagging. And I'd like to know how many others were on Meadow's list. Never mind that, though. What is perfectly clear is that Meadow got cold feet when Scorpe had a go at him during the inquest. He put out no more prescriptions.'

'Yes, but . . .'

'But what?'

'I thought Meadow was supposed to have blamed that herb stuff for what happened to Winge.'

'So he did—in public. But he didn't believe it. If he had, he wouldn't have stopped issuing his own prescriptions. He knew what Heineman was talking about, all right, and it scared him.'

There was a knock on the door. The head of Detective Constable Pook appeared.

'Come in, Mr Pook, come in. What have you got to tell us?'

Pook stepped carefully and quietly to the desk, ran his eye quickly over the hand-written foolscap sheet he was holding, and delivered it to Purbright with a little flourish.

'Miss Loder's statement, sir.'

'Ah, yes.' The inspector began to read Pook's round, painstaking script. He had that expression of calm approval which schoolmasters learn to adopt lest they discourage the thick but eager pupil.

Soon, however, the feigned interest became genuine. It livened into urgent concern. He read quickly to the end, then darted back to earlier passages, re-reading, checking.

He looked back at Love.

'You didn't tell me this girl works at the Meadow's place.'

The sergeant stared incredulously. 'She doesn't!'

'Oh, yes, she does. She was on her way to post some letters for Mrs Meadow when she got jumped.'

Purbright turned to Pook, on whose stiff, stern face was a faint flush of pride.

'She was quite sure, was she, that there was nothing sexual about the assault? I mean, she would know—she's not dim or anything?'

'No, sir. Quite intelligent, I thought.'

'He just grabbed her arm'—Purbright glanced down at the report—'and shoved her into the hedge. That's the hedge near the post box, is it?'

'Yes, sir. It runs along by the Goodacres' front garden. It's the tall, yellowish one, rather neglected.'

'I know.'

The inspector read aloud: *'He did not do anything more to me. I was frightened and a bit scratched with being pushed into the hedge. I was lying half through it and I could not get up at first. It took me perhaps half a minute to get up. The man had gone. I had heard a car. I think it must have been the car he had been hiding behind when I came along. I picked up the letters which I had dropped. I posted them and went back to Mrs Meadow's.'*

There was a pause.

'Those letters,' Purbright said. 'Did she say if any were missing?'

'No, sir.' Pook sounded a little querulous.

'Well, he must have had *some* reason for knocking her over, mustn't he?'

'But surely, sir, it's the same fellow who's been doing this sort of thing all over the place.'

'I doubt it. This man was waiting for her. He knew where to wait—by the post box nearest her employer's house. And he made no attempt to molest her sexually. Another thing—she says here that he'd pulled a scarf up over his face. That's not in line with the other cases. Then there's her description of him, such as it is . . . *middle-aged, powerful build, movements very quick.* . . . None of the other women saw anybody like that, did they, sergeant?'

Love started, then said no—no, they hadn't.

Purbright continued to look at him, brows raised, happier now, inviting the sergeant to share his cheerfulness.

'You see? Meadow. Always back to Meadow, always this link. And you talk about natural causes, sergeant?'

He lifted the phone. 'Get me Flaxborough nine-three-six-three, will you, please. I shall want to speak to a young woman called Pauline Sutton, if she is there.'

Pook silently and respectfully bobbed his farewells and tiptoed from the room. As he was closing the door behind him, he heard the inspector greet Miss Sutton with considerable geniality. Now what? Pook said bitterly to himself. He was a grudging man.

'You may remember, Pauline,' Purbright was saying, 'that there was some conversation yesterday evening between you and Mr Brennan concerning letters. I was not eavesdropping, you understand, but I did overhear the odd word. Now then, something has happened which may make what you were saying very important. I want you now to repeat it to me as precisely as you can recall it. . . .'

CHAPTER SIXTEEN

Old Dr James stood at the window of the front office of Sparrow, Sparrow and Amblesby, solicitors, and stared gloomily at a passing parade of cars. It was the funeral procession of Alderman Winge.

After the big square hearse, canopied with flowers and driven by a long, top-hatted man with a statuesque dedication that seemed quite unconnected with the vehicle's mechanical controls, came three black limousines. Exactly identical with one another, they bore the same family resemblance to the hearse, whose pace they emulated like obedient sons, as, curiously enough, did their drivers to the petrified personage in the lead.

Following the limousines were two or three less opulent but still fairly expensive cars. Thereafter, the mourners' transport became progressively less splendid —presumably in ratio to the standing and expectations of the occupants—until it terminated in the regrettable presence of the travel-stained baker's van of some third cousins from Cardiff.

Dr James shook his head. He remembered the days of plumed horses and rows of bare-headed, silent spectators.

'Poor old Steve Winge,' he said, partly to himself, partly to the two men who stood behind him. 'There was a time when the whole council would turn out to see an alderman off. They'd have followed on foot. Robes. The Mace. I wonder sometimes what has happened to our sense of occasion.'

He turned round.

'Sad. Don't you think so, Thompson?'

The deputy coroner looked up from fiddling with a key ring and said yes, he did think it was sad, funerals nowadays were little better than disposal parties.

Sergeant Malley, who unwillingly half-filled what little space had been left in the little office by a welter of Victorian lawyers' furniture, hoped that this sort of talk would not go on much longer. The inspector, he knew, was in an oddly impatient frame of mind; he wasn't going to relish the news that after taking a look at Meadow's body old James had blithely signed a certificate of natural death.

'You'll not recall,' Dr James was saying, 'when Bert Amblesby took over as coroner.'

It was a safe statement. Neither Malley nor Thompson had even been born at that remote remove of time.

'His partner, Zeke Sparrow, died the following year, and, do you know, there was black crepe all the way down the High Street. Fourteen carriages. Think of that.'

'People don't have the time any more,' said Thompson. He was thinking that he was running a bit short of that commodity himself just then.

'Time? It's respect they lack, not time. Did you notice what was happening out there?' Dr James indicated the window with a nod of his silver-white head. 'There were cars overtaking and cutting in. One actually hooted at the hearse.'

The sergeant stole a look at his watch. Strictly speaking, he was at the disposal of the deputy coroner, but

Thompson seemed to lack courage to break away from the reminiscences of his elderly colleague. That was the trouble with doctors, Malley told himself. They'd cheerfully knife one another at a safe distance, but as long as an outsider was looking on they were too busy being mutually respectful to bloody breathe.

'Shocking business, young Meadow passing away like that,' observed Dr James. It was the fourth time he had made the remark since he had held a mirror that morning to the lips of the peaceful and still handsome corpse in the hospital morgue and murmured: 'Gone, by Jove—not a glimmer.'

Dr Thompson's sigh was a fraction too vigorous to have been prompted by sympathy, but old James did not appear to notice.

'Better than lingering after a stroke, though, some might say. I don't know. Very difficult question. My word—what a cramped little office this is. Don't you find it cramped, eh? I'll bet the sergeant here does.' Unexpectedly, the old man grinned.

Malley smiled back and seized his opportunity.

'I rather think they'll be expecting me back at Fen Street,' he said quietly to Thompson, 'but there is just one thing, sir, I'd like to be clear about when I see the inspector.'

'And what is that, sergeant?'

The deputy coroner, too, had lowered his voice. He was nervous lest anything they said should elicit further reminiscence from old James.

'I take it as definitely your opinion that there shouldn't be an inquest. Is that right, sir?'

Thompson stiffened. 'Of course it's right. Why shouldn't it be?'

'I just wanted to be sure, sir.'

Dr James glanced sharply across at them.

'Sure about what?'

'Nothing, doctor. The sergeant was only asking if we had any other cases to be dealt with today.'

'He said something about an inquest,' persisted the old man. 'Why should there be an inquest? I've signed a certificate, haven't I?' His head was rocking gently up and down, as if he had some machinery inside him.

'As long as you're satisfied, doctor,' said Malley, easily.

He peered inside his cap, adjusted its shape a little, and put it on. The cap was not quite big enough and he had to pull it well forward and down to conform with the Chief Constable's dictum that no policeman could do his job properly unless the tip of his cap peak were in line with, and equidistant from his ear lobes.

Dr James stared at the result and mistook for insolent indifference the sergeant's resemblance to a patient, blinkered carthorse.

'I should like to know just what you are insinuating, officer. If it is suggested that after fifty-two years in general practice . . .'

'Oh, come now, doctor,' Thompson interjected. 'I'm sure my officer would not dream of calling your judgment into doubt. He simply has to report the facts to his inspector, and he wishes to be absolutely accurate. Isn't that so, Malley?'

'Of course, sir,' said the horse.

Dr James simmered silently a few moments longer, then made a determined effort to stop nodding.

'Very well, then. But don't let us hear any more talk about inquests. That won't do anybody any good. It's a sad enough business as it is. Great loss to the profession. And to the town.'

He stared out once more through the small, dusty

panes of the window, as though to see how the town was taking it.

'Indeed yes,' murmured Dr Thompson. Surreptitiously he gave Malley a nudge to signify that he'd better go while the going was good.

In another lawyer's office, Inspector Purbright was cheerfully telling Mr Scorpe that he proposed to be so shamelessly unethical as to try and pick that gentleman's brains.

Since his talk over the telephone with Pauline Sutton, Purbright had been feeling a good deal more energetic. New hope engendered a pleasant recklessness.

Mr Scorpe at first looked startled. Then he lowered the angle of his long wooden face and gazed over his spectacles with a touch of amusement.

'You are being very frank, inspector.'

'Not frank. Downright impertinent. I want you to tell me what the analyst found in that sample of herbs you sent off to him.'

Scorpe pulled a tray of letters across the desk top and began sorting through them.

'Go away,' he said.

'Come along, you can afford to do me a favour. And this one won't cost you anything.'

'What gives you the idea'—Scorpe did not raise his eyes—'that I should have wanted something analysing? This isn't a forensic science agency.'

'No, but you're acting for the Winges, and we all know *their* family motto—"Somebody's Got to be Summonsed". Moldham Meres Laboratories will do as well as anyone else.'

'Really, inspector! That is a most improper suggestion!'

'Yes, isn't it?'

Purbright put his head on one side and gently scratched his ear.

'What did they find?'

Scorpe turned over another couple of letters.

'You get your own analysing done,' he said, gruffly. 'My client has to pay. Yours don't.'

'Aye, but it's a question of saving time. You wouldn't mind doing that for me, I know.'

Scorpe remained for half a minute in silent examination of his correspondence. Then, without looking, he opened and reached into a drawer and held out a small sheet of buff-coloured paper. Purbright took it.

The report was short. It referred to inert vegetable matter, minimal water content, insignificant mineral traces, non-toxic alkaloids, all derived from a plant of the genus Compositae, probably Taraxacum Officinale, or the common dandelion.

'Hard luck,' said Purbright. He put the sheet back into the still extended hand of Mr Scorpe.

'You haven't seen me,' said the solicitor, feeling for the drawer.

Purbright made his way through Priory Lane to the river end of East Street and went into the Roebuck. After drinking half a pint of bitter in the deserted public bar, he sought out the manager, Mr Maddox, and asked him if a gentleman named Brennan was still among his guests.

The manager's morning frown deepened. He looked at the register, then behind him at the key board.

'He is, yes. Did you want to see him?'

'Not at the moment. Has he given any indication of how long he intends to stay?'

'He's booked until the day after tomorrow.'

'Right. If he changes his plans, I shall be glad if you will telephone at once and let us know, Mr Maddox. It's very important.'

'I trust there's nothing, ah . . .'

Long experience of the contingencies of the hotel trade had instilled in Mr Maddox a chronic anxiety, attested by his apparent inability to finish a sentence. Moreover, whenever he said "I trust . . ."—which was very often—he meant exactly the opposite.

'No, no, nothing,' said Purbright, airily.

'The fact is, we've had two already this week who haven't, ah . . .'

'Have you, indeed?'

'Mr Brennan didn't strike me as that sort, actually.'

'Oh? As what sort *did* he strike you?'

'Rather gentlemanly for a commercial. If he is one, that is. I've not noticed him playing billiards, come to think of it, although I suppose that's not, er . . .'

'Did you happen to notice at what time he came in last night?'

'Ye-es, it would be about, oh, nine, quarter-past nine.'

'How was he dressed?'

Maddox shook his head doubtfully.

'That I couldn't really say. I think he was carrying a coat . . . no, I'm wrong—I was thinking of someone else. He's got his own car here, you know. Or is it hired? Yes, I remember he asked about hiring when he arrived. Simpsons probably, ah . . . Or the Two-Star, perhaps. It's a grey Hillman, anyway.'

'You say you did see him come in last night. Did you see anything of a scarf?'

At this question, which Maddox obviously considered to have sinister overtones, his expression changed to one of alarm.

'I do feel, inspector, that for the sake of the hotel, you should say if there's anything, ah . . .'

Purbright assured him at once that he had no need to feel apprehensive. To the truthful assertion that nothing was known to Mr Brennan's discredit, he added, less truthfully: 'We are only trying to eliminate him from an inquiry that's been going on.'

'I see,' said the manager. 'Well, that's all right, then. A scarf, you say. . . . No, I've never seen him wearing a scarf.'

'What room is he in?'

'Twenty-seven.'

'And he's in it now?'

Maddox again consulted the key board. 'Yes.'

'In that case, I wonder if you'd mind coming outside and showing me which is his car.'

At the back of the hotel was a walled area that once had been the coaching yard. Part of it was still paved with cobblestones. Above the broad archway that divided the hotel's ground floor and gave access to the street, there survived a balustraded balcony from which guests of two hundred years before had watched ostlers hasten to tend the steaming horses that had drawn the "Nottingham Flyer" or the "Eastern Mail".

Purbright looked up at the balcony and at the windows above. 'Is there any chance of his spotting us down here?'

'No, twenty-seven is on the far side. In any case, the residents' cars are kept under cover. I'll show you.'

He led the way to a roofed enclosure. There were ten or a dozen cars inside. Maddox pointed to one of them and then turned to stand facing the yard.

Brennan's car was locked. Purbright made a note of its number, then circled the car, peering through the windows. On the back seat were two leather cases, one small, the other about the size of a suitcase. Both were square and rigid-looking; designed, Purbright imagined, to hold pharmaceutical or surgical samples. He did not see the briefcase he had noticed Brennan carrying in the surgery. Several Elixon leaflets were in evidence, though.

On the front passenger seat was a rolled-up raincoat. It was a very pale mushroom colour; in better light, it would look practically white. Purbright scrutinized the coat from as many angles as he could by pressing his face against the glass and shielding off reflections with his hands. From one position he succeeded in spotting a tuck of some darker material. Something—possibly a thin scarf or silk square—had been rolled within the coat.

He rejoined Maddox, whom he thanked and again adjured to make instant report of any sign of his guest's intentions to depart. Then he set off for the other end of town and Heston Lane.

How deeply grieved was Mrs Meadow by her husband's death, Purbright found difficult at first sight to decide. What was certain was that he encountered a woman monumentally put out.

His condolences were received with a formality just short of indifference. He had put no more than three questions before she shook her head impatiently.

'I'm sorry, inspector, but if you really must know these things, you will have to ask someone else. Perhaps my husband's solicitor could find time to help you.'

'I doubt if that would meet the case, Mrs Meadow. You must believe me when I say that I am trying to spare you as much distress and inconvenience as I can.

But there are some questions—they will not take long, I promise you—which you alone can answer.'

Grudgingly, she relaxed slightly the attitude of preparing to get up from her chair.

'I asked you a moment ago,' Purbright resumed, 'where the doctor was yesterday between, say, five o'clock and six, when he went into surgery.'

'He was here, naturally. We always have tea served at four-thirty.'

'Did he not go out at any time during that hour?'

'No.'

'And was there no one else in the house, apart from yourself?'

'Only the maid.'

'Elizabeth Loder?'

She looked at him narrowly.

'I don't see why you should know her name . . . Oh, the business down the road, of course. I hope nothing's going to be made of that, by the way. Not on top of everything else. The girl wasn't hurt, you know.'

'No,' said Purbright. 'She wasn't.' He thought for a moment, then asked: 'Did anyone call on the doctor yesterday afternoon?'

'I don't think so. He was across at the office for most of the afternoon. Until about half-past four. No, I'm sure no one called.'

'So he had no contact with anyone other than you or Miss Loder from four-thirty until he left the house at six.'

'Ten to six,' she corrected. 'The patients begin to be seen at six, but my husband always went over ten or fifteen minutes beforehand.'

'Might he have had a caller during that time?'

'Yesterday evening, you mean?'

'Yes.'

'It's possible. . . . But really, inspector. I don't get the drift of all this.'

Purbright delved for what might serve as a plausible explanation.

'I'm sorry. The fact is that we believe that the man who attacked Miss Loder might have been hanging round the house or the surgery earlier in the day.'

'Miss Loder . . . ? Oh, you mean Elizabeth. But surely you're not taking up all this time and asking me all these odd questions because of that? It was a very trivial incident.'

'There have been other attacks, Mrs Meadow.'

'There might have been, but that doesn't mean my house should be flooded with policemen. Especially at a time like this. Tell me, does Mr Chubb know you're here?'

'The Chief Constable is aware that inquiries are being made,' Purbright said, stiffly.

Mrs Meadow gave a short nod. 'I think I shall have to have a word with him.'

'Very good. But if I might take advantage of your forbearance for one moment more, Mrs Meadow, I should like just to be a little clearer about the period we were discussing. Can you suggest—and I assure you that this is important—anyone at all who may have visited the doctor between ten minutes to six yesterday evening and six o'clock when the surgery opened?'

Despite her expression of bleak resentment, she did appear to give the question thought.

After a while, she said: 'There is one possibility, although I'm sure it is irrelevant. My husband had been writing an article for professional publication. He finished it yesterday. Apparently it made reference to the effects of some drug or other, and I believe Dr Meadow intended to show the article to the representative of a firm—one of the leading pharmaceutical firms—for which he had been doing research. He may—and I say *may*—have seen this man before surgery. It was a period he set aside for dealing with travellers and people like that. So that his patients would not be inconvenienced, you understand.'

She stood up.

'That is all I can tell you, inspector. And now you must please excuse me. Elizabeth will see you out.'

She picked up a little ornamental handbell and, somewhat to the inspector's embarrassment, shook it resolutely.

Purbright waited until the girl was about to open the front door before he spoke to her.

'Hang on a minute, Elizabeth. Just a couple of quick questions about what happened to you yesterday.'

She looked at him nervously, then glanced back down the hall.

'I don't know that I ought, really . . . she says I'm not to make any fuss about it.'

'I shan't keep you a second.'

'But the policeman who came—he wrote everything down, I told it all to him.' She kept one slim, brown hand on the door catch.

'The car the man was hiding behind—I don't think you described that, did you?'

'I didn't notice it, really.'

'Not the colour, even?'

'I think it was a sort of greyish colour.' Again she looked past him, towards the room containing Mrs Meadow and her bell.

'I see. Make? Number? No good?'

She shook her head.

'Never mind. Now the man. His face was covered. In something brown, you said. Something patterned? Or not.'

'Patterned, I think.'

'And his coat. You said white. Are you sure?'

'Yes, white. It was thin and sort of smooth.'

'Have you ever seen a continental raincoat, Elizabeth? The sort they wear in Germany, Scandinavia, places like that?'

'No, I don't think so.'

'The letters. Now I want you to think very carefully. When you picked them up again, are you sure they were all there?'

'Please—I'll have to be getting back . . .' She turned her face and began opening the door, but not quickly enough to hide sudden flushed cheeks.

Purbright touched her arm.

'How many were missing, Elizabeth? It's very important that I know.'

'One. Only one. I . . . I daren't let on about it. She'd have got mad at me.'

'Do you know which one? Had you seen the address on it?'

'Somewhere in London, I think. It was one of those long envelopes, and it had more stamps on than the others. You won't let her know, will you?'

'Typewritten?'

The girl nodded miserably.

'Listen,' said Purbright. 'Does this sound familiar? The British . . .' He formed his lips into the pronunciation of an M, and waited.

Suddenly she brightened, her unhappiness dispelled for the moment by a chance to show herself clever.

'British Medical Journal! Yes, that was it. I'm sure it was.'

'Good girl,' said Purbright. He pulled open the door himself and stepped through.

Sergeant Malley, gingerly carrying a brimful mug of tea from the canteen back to his office, raised his head to see Purbright immediately in front of him. He stopped. A little of the tea slopped on the corridor floor. The inspector was looking so cheerful that Malley had to remind himself that Purbright was not by nature a rib-poker before he felt safe to squeeze to one side and give him room to pass.

'Oh, about Meadow . . .' he began.

'Have they done the autopsy yet?' the inspector interrupted eagerly.

'Autopsy?'

'Certainly. Have you not seen Heineman yet?'

Malley gripped his mug more firmly. 'I have, as a matter of fact. Thompson, too. And Dr James. There isn't going to be any autopsy.'

Purbright stared. 'What the hell are they playing at?'

'Thompson's decided that there's no need for an inquest. James signed a certificate, so it looks as though that's that.'

'That is bloody well not that! Come on, Bill—get into your office. I'll phone from there.'

Dr Thompson had left Sparrow, Sparrow and Amblesby. Purbright tried the deputy coroner's own home. Mrs Thompson suggested the doctor might have driven over to the hospital. He had his medical duties to perform as well, the inspector would realize. She plainly shared her husband's opinion that the honour of deputizing for old Amblesby was not worth the trouble involved.

The matron at the General said that Dr Thompson

had gone on the wards to visit one of his patients. She would have him called to a telephone.

Purbright waited restlessly, weighing the receiver in his hand.

'I know what it is,' he said to Malley. 'Doctors. Mutual protection association.'

The sergeant pushed his tea carefully to one side to make room for a tin of tobacco.

'I think you'll find Heineman's the trouble. The G.P.s don't like pathologists much anyway—they spot the mistakes after the damage has been done—and Heinie's an outsider. He's only been here eleven years. You can imagine what the feeling is going to be when it's not just a patient but one of the fraternity who goes on his slab.'

'Aye, but Meadow was murdered, Bill. I'm absolutely positive now.'

Malley paused in sniffing his newly opened tin.

'How?'

'God knows. That's the hell of it. But it was done. Somehow or other it was done.'

'And do you know who did it?' Beneath Malley's bucolic manner was now a tense seriousness.

'Aye,' said Purbright, and left it at that.

A series of loud clicks came from the phone, followed by a voice, querulous, irritable.

Purbright spoke.

'Dr Thompson? Inspector Purbright . . . Yes, I realize that. I'm sorry. But this is urgent. I understand from the coroner's officer that you have decided against holding an inquest on Dr Meadow . . .'

Four minutes later, Purbright put down the receiver and faced Malley with an expression of stony anger.

The sergeant removed his pipe and glanced with mild curiosity into the bowl.

'No joy?'

'He can see no reason for what he calls impugning the judgment of a competent and highly respected physician. That's what he thinks his order for a P.M. would amount to.'

Malley took an experimental suck at his pipe and looked again in the bowl. 'I was rather afraid you'd not be able to convince him.'

'Evidence—give me evidence, he says, that a crime's been committed. But, God almighty, the only evidence we can ever hope to find is in that bloke's belly. So what am I supposed to do?'

'Difficult,' said Malley, between puffs. 'Pity there can't be a little misunderstanding. I mean, Heinie would be in there filleting before anyone could stop him, once he got the word. . . .'

'Oh, no!' Purbright held up his hand. 'You can stop thinking along those lines, Bill. Pirate autopsies are definitely out.'

'What are you going to do, then?'

Purbright lay back in his chair and stared disconsolately at the wall. For a long time, he said nothing. What he did murmur at last made sense neither to the sergeant nor to himself.

' "The fur is darker".'

CHAPTER SEVENTEEN

'I believe you have a Mr Brennan staying here. I should like to see him, please.'

The girl with the black fringe and a deep absorption in a magazine reached in slow motion for the house phone without looking up. 'What name, madam?'

'Mr Brennan.'

'No madam—*your* name.'

'My name is Miss Teatime.'

The girl set a plump white finger-end to guard the last word she had read, and peeked suspiciously through her fringe. Then, with the same hand that held the phone, she contrived to push home one of the switchboard plugs.

'There's a lady in reception to see you, sir. She says her name is Miss Teatime.'

The girl listened, looking fixedly at the visitor.

'Very good, sir.'

She removed the plug, seated the phone, and made rendezvous with the waiting finger.

'Room twenty-seven, madam.'

Miss Teatime walked to the lift.

On the second floor, the door of twenty-seven already stood open.

Brennan, who now wore a brown suit that made

him look bulkier than when she had seen him last, was on the threshold. He watched Miss Teatime's approach along the corridor with an expression of curiosity, interrupted occasionally by a downward glance at the progress of something he was doing with his hands. As she got nearer, she saw that he was peeling an apple. He managed it very expertly so that the peel hung unbroken in a long green and white spiral which gently rose and fell as the apple turned beneath the knife.

'Good evening, Mr Brennan.'

He made a short bow, saying nothing, and stood back from the doorway.

Miss Teatime entered the room.

'We have met, you know.'

'Yes. Yes, of course.'

He let fall the appleskin coil neatly into an ornamental wastepaper tub beside the fireplace. The pocketing of the penknife was the conclusion of a single sweeping motion that brought the back of the blade against his thigh, snapping it shut. All his actions, Miss Teatime thought, would be like that—accurate, economical.

'Please . . .' He pointed to a chair.

She sat. Brennan remained standing by the table, on which he had laid his peeled apple on a saucer. He regarded her with polite expectancy.

As Miss Teatime removed a pair of light fawn gloves, she made a quick survey of the room; not inquisitively, but in the manner of a well-bred guest sizing up an agreeable situation. She saw that it was not a self-contained room, with a bed, like most of those at the Roebuck, but one from which two doors led to other apartments, presumably bathroom and bedroom. The carpet, a blue Wilton, was comparatively new, and the furniture included an antique lacquered cabinet, a pair of good chairs and a small bureau in reproduction Chippendale style. A big console television set supervised the room from one corner. By Flaxborough standards, it was all rather grand.

'And what can I do for you, Miss Teatime?'

She turned upon him her full attention, graced with a friendly smile.

'My errand will probably surprise you, but the fact is that I have come to make application for a grant.'

He frowned. 'I don't think I quite . . .'

'No, of course not. You cannot be expected to understand until I tell you who I am, can you? I am, so to speak, Moldham Meres Laboratories. That is to say, I am the company's managing director—not,' she added hastily, 'that I would like you to think of me as a tycoon or anything of that kind; we are a small and highly specialized concern, and it just happens that major responsibility has fallen upon me because of my long experience—through social work, you know—of the needs of elderly people. I do not need to remind you, of course that the geriatric field is the area to which Moldham Meres Laboratories make particular contribution.'

'I can scarcely be reminded,' said Brennan, 'of something I wasn't aware of in the first place. I'm afraid I have never heard of these laboratories of yours.'

Miss Teatime looked shocked, but only for an instant. She good-humouredly wagged an admonitory finger.

'Now, Mr Brennan, we must not allow commercial rivalry to dictate our attitudes, must we? Human welfare is our common concern. Let us not pretend blindness to each other's existence as workers towards that end.'

'I have not heard of your firm,' Brennan repeated. 'And I am at a loss to understand what you said earlier about your purpose in coming to see me. A grant? What grant? How can you imagine that I have anything to do with grants?'

'You are the representative,' Miss Teatime resumed patiently, 'of the West German drug house of Elixon, are you not?'

'Certainly.'

'And Elixon entertain high hopes that the product they allow to be made under licence here and marketed as "Juniform" will prove a very valuable aid to geriatricians.'

'I would rather not discuss my firm's products otherwise than with professional people, if you don't mind.'

'Oh, but I am not discussing them. I stated a fact which I assume to be available to anyone who cares to read the medical press.'

'Is that where you heard about "Juniform"?'

'No.'

'Where, then?'

'You forget, Mr Brennan. We are fellow toilers in the vineyard of human advancement. The only difference is that whereas your remedies are drawn from the retort and the centrifuge, mine rise directly from the earth.'

'Very picturesque.'

'Yes, but allow me to continue what I was saying. This "Juniform", if it lived up to its promise, could be a tremendously significant drug. As I understand your firm's admirably restrained claims, "Juniform" actually holds back the effects of old age.'

'That is nowhere stated by us.'

'Not in those words, perhaps. "Inhibits the onset of cellular modifications associated with the ageing process." That seems to me to be very much the same thing. No matter—what your firm is offering is nothing more or less than a modern version of the great prize sought by the ancients, the Elixir of Life. I'm sorry—am I being picturesque again?'

'You are employing a silly and sensational catch-phrase.'

'Solely to illustrate my point that "Juniform" has sensational commercial possibilities. Always provided' —she put her fingertips together and regarded them critically—'that it produces no nasty side-effects.'

Brennan, who had remained standing in exactly the same position since Miss Teatime's arrival in the room, took out and slickly opened his penknife. He picked up the apple, which was already brown-mottled by exposure, and with a deft, twisting incision, levered a piece out and carried it between thumb and knife blade to his mouth.

Miss Teatime was interested to see that he could eat with scarcely any overt jaw movement. She wondered if, instead of using his teeth, he had acquired the ability to crush food between his tongue and the roof of his mouth.

'Oh, but I must not frighten you with talk of side-effects. I know they are bound to be a constant nightmare for you pharmaceutical people, and I do sympathize with you. Well, I know what I should feel if we began to receive complaints at Moldham Meres that people had been taken ill after using our products.'

Brennan cut away another piece of apple. There was a slightly more savage turn of the twist this time. He remained silent.

'To tell you the truth,' Miss Teatime continued in a lowered voice, 'and quite in confidence between ourselves, there *have* been one or two cases lately that give me concern. A somewhat curious illness has afflicted several of our customers. Moreover'—her voice fell still further—'there has been publicity. You may well imagine how damaging *that* can be.

'The odd thing is that every one of these unfortunate customers of ours happens, or happened (one of them has died, I fear), to be also a taker of "Juniform". This doubtless is pure coincidence, but it may serve to help you appreciate my firm's predicament. I mean, it does bring you closer to the problem, does it not?'

She frowned. 'Now, what was the other strange coincidence I meant to mention? Ah, yes—this illness. Do you know, it is exactly similar—or so I am reliably informed—to one that has been reported in a couple of Continental countries. And yet Moldham Meres Laboratories do not sell any of their products in Europe. I find that comforting, I must say, but it *is* rather mysterious.'

The apple was now sculpted down to its core. Brennan regarded the remnant pensively for a moment, then placed it on the saucer.

'And why are you telling me all this?' He spoke with tight, cold precision.

'Because I dared to hope that you might be interested in the problem as a colleague.'

'That is nonsense. What have I to do with this . . . this nature cure chicanery?'

'Let us not use harsh words. Mr Brennan. I am simply giving you an opportunity to use your influence with a very worthy organization towards an equally worthy end.'

'Again nonsense! My dear woman, if you imagine . . .'

'Please do not tell me,' Miss Teatime interrupted firmly, 'that you are unaware of the existence of C.I.R.F.'

'And what is that pray?' Behind the hard, sardonic tone, there was a hint of caution.

'The Chemo-therapy International Research Foundation, Mr Brennan.'

'Ye-es, I have heard of it.'

'You should have done. It happens to be the creation of your own firm, by which it continues to be financed.'

'What of it?'

'The funds of C.I.R.F.—and please correct me if I am wrong to believe them substantial—are used to finance clinical trials of new drugs. They are supposed to be administered impartially, and I am sure they are, but the only trials of which I have personal knowledge are those which Dr Meadow—the late Dr Meadow, rather—conducted on "Juniform". Dr Meadow received grants from the Foundation totalling nearly six thousand pounds. It was money well spent, of course, because it enabled him to establish that the drug was not only efficacious but completely harmless. His findings were published in the medical press and went into the sales literature of Elixon to be distributed all over the world.'

Brennan walked slowly to a chair and sat down. He did not take his eyes off her, nor, even when seated, did he relax the military stiffness of his back and shoulders.

'Go on, Miss Teatime.'

She nodded and gave him a benign smile.

'How fortunate that poor Dr Meadow was spared

to complete his work in time. But now, alas, he has gone, and one might almost say that a vacancy has arisen in consequence.'

'A vacancy?'

'Yes—in relation to the availability of C.I.R.F. funds, I mean. Forgive my being forthright—presumptuous, I fear, was my father's word for it—Sir William Teatime, the surgeon, you know—but it did occur to me that a research grant might appropriately be made to Moldham Meres Laboratories, in view of the parallel nature of our work in geriatrics. After all'—Miss Teatime gave a little shrug of sweet reasonableness—'my firm *did* receive the blame for those regrettable cases of indisposition which might just as well have been caused by "Juniform", despite Dr Meadow's vigilance.'

For a long time Brennan's square, sombre face remained quite motionless while he stared unblinkingly at Miss Teatime. Then he gave a curt nod, as if he had just made up his mind about something, and examined his hands, slowly bending and unbending the stubby, powerful fingers.

'When you came in here,' he said, 'I thought you were a crazy but harmless old woman . . .'

'That was a most ungentlemanly impression!'

Brennan ignored the interruption. '. . . but I see now that you are clever and far from harmless. It is obvious that you have been making a lot of inquiries into matters which cannot be said to concern you. You think you have found things out which will embarrass me or the firm I represent. Perhaps—and I shall put it no more strongly than this, out of respect for your age and sex—you are hopeful of financial gain.'

'Perish,' stoutly interjected Miss Teatime, 'the thought!'

'Ah, I am glad to hear you say so. Because, believe me, you will be damnably disappointed'—his voice suddenly rose to a shout—'damnably disappointed, I say!—if you imagine that I will tolerate, let alone succumb to, any threat from you!'

Miss Teatime's small, dainty mouth pursed in conjecture.

'You know, Mr Brennan, there is something about you which I do not quite understand. You do not have the style of a commercial traveller. Nor do you speak like one. I am particularly intrigued, because your name is not known at the London office of Elixon's subsidiary company in England.'

He glared. 'My God! Your spying seems to have been very thorough!'

'My inquiries,' she corrected, gently.

'You will stop interrupting! Let me make this absolutely clear. Unless you cease your preposterous attempt to extort money and leave here immediately, I shall send for the manager and have you removed.'

'That would be very unethical, Mr Brennan. I have done no more than put to you a reasonable suggestion concerning medical research.'

'Get out!'

He had risen from his chair and was now standing a few feet away from her. His brittle fury was like that of a parade ground officer faced with some insolent subordinate.

Miss Teatime did not budge. She smoothed out a small crease in her skirt, sat a little more erect, and shook her head regretfully.

'Oh, dear. So Germanic.'

'What do you mean by that?'

'You certainly could not be accused of having a bedside manner, doctor. But then, general practice is not your sphere, is it?'

'You are a lunatic! I was right, after all. You are mad as a hatmaker!'

She laughed. '*Hutmacher* . . . no, no, you are too carefully colloquial, doctor. In England, we say hatter. Nevertheless, your accent is most creditable—apart from a certain residual flatness. Tell me, how long were you in South Africa after the war, Dr Brunnen?'

He walked to the door, opened it, and came back to stand over Miss Teatime. She felt his fingers close over her upper arm.

'If you would be so good, madam . . .'

The harsh, ironic voice was within an inch or two of her ear. She was aware of her shoulder rising as if it had been trapped in machinery. For a second, the rest of her body drooped helplessly from it, like that of a cat picked up by one foreleg.

Brennan took a step towards the door.

Inexplicably, his foot failed to meet the ground. It seemed to have been taken in charge with quite astonishing dexterity and determination by Miss Teatime, who, slipping from his grasp, now thrust herself neatly aside so as not to impede Brennan's floorward plunge.

The room reverberated so violently that it was some little time before the ringing of the telephone separated out as a significant sound.

Brennan lifted his head. Ponderously, he raised himself to a kneeling position.

Miss Teatime looked down at him sternly.

'You must never do that again,' she said.

The phone was ringing once more.

'Are you not going to answer it?'

Brennan got to his feet. He steadied himself against the wall and picked up the phone.

While he listened, he scowled with increasing intensity at Miss Teatime.

'Yes, I see. . . . Did they say why? . . . No, I'll come down. Tell them that. I shall be down in a moment, yes.'

Back went the receiver. The baleful stare was maintained.

'More of your stupid nonsense?'

'I beg your pardon?'

'Those two policemen downstairs. They are your idea?'

'They most assuredly are not!'

Miss Teatime's indignation had the ring of truth.

Brennan turned and hurried from the room.

Following as far as the door, Miss Teatime watched him walk swiftly to the end of the corridor and go from sight round the corner. To the right. But the lift, she remembered, was on the left. He must have chosen to descend by the staircase.

She went back into the room and opened the front of the lacquered cabinet. It contained only a couple of bottles, a soda syphon and several glasses.

Two of the three drawers in the bureau were empty. In the third were hotel stationery, a pen, a map, rubber bands, an electric light bulb.

She made rapid search of the bathroom, paying special attention to a ventilator shutter and to the inside of the flushing cistern. In neither had anything been concealed. She pulled the door shut after her and went to work on the bedroom.

To the contents of the two small cupboards and the bedside locker, Miss Teatime paid only fleeting attention. She spent longer feeling between the clothing stacked with meticulous tidiness in a chest of drawers and explored the least obvious recesses within the big built-in wardrobe.

Then, as she stood by the bed, about to lift a corner of the mattress, she caught the sound of voices. At once, she slipped back into the main room.

Purbright appeared at the open door. Behind his shoulder hung the amiable, inquisitive face of Love, like a rosy moon.

'What on earth are *you* doing here? Where's Brennan?'

'I presume you want an answer to the second question first. Mr Brennan left this room about three minutes ago. He said he was going down to see you.'

'Well, he didn't. Sergeant—go and keep an eye on his car. It should be in the garage at the back. Grey Hillman, HMU-something-or-other.'

Love's face dipped, then floated away.

'May I invite you in, inspector, on Mr Brennan's behalf? I cannot think he's likely to be far off.'

Purbright entered. He pushed the door nearly shut.

'And now your answer to the first question.'

'Why I am here? I came to persuade Mr Brennan of the error of his ways.'

'Which particular ways, Miss Teatime?'

'You should know, inspector. Otherwise, why should you be here yourself?'

'Ah, now you know better than to imagine that I am going to barter motives. Policemen have one great advantage, they need never account for their presence anywhere.'

'If I found one in my bath, I fancy I should be entitled to an explanation.'

'Not if he were in uniform. But you are not bathing at the moment, Miss Teatime, and I must not waste time in chat. Where is Brennan?'

Suddenly her expression changed.

'What is it you wish to question Mr Brennan about?'

'Oh, come now, Miss Teatime!'

'This is not mere inquisitiveness, and I do not mean to sound impertinent. Please tell me.'

He regarded her in silence for a moment.

'Very well. I want to ask him what he knows about an assault that took place the other night.'

'A criminal assault?'

'No. Technically, a common assault.'

She nodded. 'Not a felony, then. Not an indictable offence at all. So you have no power to arrest him.'

'That's true.'

She smiled at him slowly. 'You do not much care do you, inspector, for the exercise known as making bricks without straw.'

He, too, smiled. 'Not greatly, no.'

'I may possibly be able to provide you with a little straw. Allow me to remain and we shall see.'

The door was pushed open. Brennan, accompanied by Love, entered the room. He glanced coldly at Miss Teatime, then addressed the inspector.

'I'm sorry, I was under the impression that you had arrived by the other entrance. I have been looking for you there.'

'I met the gentleman in the yard,' Love side-remarked to Purbright.

'That's all right, Mr Brennan. The main thing is that we've finally managed to catch up with one another. I hadn't really supposed'—the inspector grinned—'that you'd gone tearing off to the nearest airport or anything like that.'

Brennan responded with a brief, thin smile.

'There is a matter,' Purbright began, 'about which we hope you might be able to give us some useful information, sir. We are investigating an incident in Heston Lane two evenings ago. The evening of the twelfth. A young woman was assaulted near a post box. You may know the place, sir—it's quite near Dr Meadow's surgery.'

'I know where the surgery is, yes.'

'Well, of course you were actually in the area not long before—as, indeed, I was myself.'

'That is true.'

'Did you happen to see or hear anything which may have a bearing on what happened to that girl?'

'No, I can't say I did. I had no reason to be particularly observant.'

'You remember no one hanging about near the letter box?'

'I'm not sure that I've ever noticed a letter box in Heston Lane. In any case, I went to and from the surgery by car. I would have been watching the road at the time.'

'At what time, sir?'

'When I was coming back. About half-past six, wasn't it, or a quarter to seven? You were there when I left the surgery.'

The inspector looked at Brennan's suit.

'Were you wearing something else that evening, Mr Brennan? My mental picture of you has some grey in it.'

'Naturally. The suit I had on then was grey.'

'You weren't wearing a coat, by any chance? Then —or later on?'

'No, I wasn't.'

'Not a light raincoat, perhaps?'

'Now look, inspector—you said you wanted to ask me some questions. Very well, I am glad to give what information I can to help the police. But I do not care to be cross-examined. Especially in front of strangers.'

Purbright looked surprised. 'This lady is a stranger to you, sir?'

'Virtually, yes. She came to see me on a matter of business.'

'But this is your room, sir. I can scarcely ask a guest of yours to leave it.'

Brennan shrugged. Miss Teatime gave him a sympathetic smile and moved over to the fireplace, where she began to examine intently a framed print of Constable's "Hay Wain".

'Now, sir, just one more question about this matter of clothes. Do you own a lightweight raincoat, very pale in colour, practically white?'

'I do not,' asserted Brennan. 'Or at least'—he carefully checked the irritation in his voice—'I never wear one. There is an old coat in the car. I keep it there in case I should need to get out in the rain.'

Purbright appeared to find this reasonable. Brennan added: 'I've had no occasion to put that coat on for, oh, at least a couple of weeks.'

Suddenly and quite sharply, the inspector asked: 'Where were you at eight o'clock that evening, sir?'

There was a short silence. Then Brennan looked over towards the fireplace.

'Miss Teatime—just a moment, if you wouldn't mind.'

She faced them.

'The inspector would like to know where I was at eight o'clock on the evening of the day before yesterday. Perhaps you would be good enough to tell him.' Without pausing, Brennan faced the inspector again. 'Her firm has been awarded a grant by one of the medical research trusts. A quite substantial grant, I understand. My own company has been asked to help with currency arrangements. I met Miss Teatime by appointment on the very evening that you happen to be talking about. A few minutes before eight o'clock, if I remember rightly.'

He looked again at Miss Teatime.

So did Purbright. Unlike Brennan's, however, his expression was one of perplexity.

Miss Teatime walked towards them a little hesitantly. She glanced from one to the other, and gave a gentle sigh.

'I am very much afraid,' she said slowly, 'that this places me in a somewhat invidious position. I must now make certain facts plain. It is quite true,' she said to Purbright, 'that a grant to my company has been mooted—a grant of . . . oh, dear, what was it? Three thousand pounds?'

Brennan nodded. 'Three thousand.'

'No, I am wrong. Four thousand. That was the figure, was it not, Mr Brennan?'

Brennan's frown seemed to indicate rapid calculation. 'Ye-es . . . more nearly four, perhaps. At the present exchange rate.'

'Thank you. Yes, as I was saying, such a grant had indeed been suggested, and my company would have been delighted to accept it, as you may imagine, inspector. But Mr Brennan has been too modest in describing his own role in the matter. You see, he is something more than a mere representative of the firm which undertook the negotiation of the grant. He is a director and a co-founder.'

Sergeant Love, who had been gazing around with a mildly bored expression, gave Brennan a respectful glance.

'Is this true, sir?' Purbright asked.

'I would rather Miss Teatime had respected my confidence,' said Brennan. 'In business, it is not always wise to advertise one's connections. However, I see no point in denying what she says.'

Purbright returned his attention to Miss Teatime.

'I am relieved,' she said, 'that this gentleman is showing such forbearance. It would be even more painful for me to be frank—and frank I must be—if I thought he might bear me ill-will. The grant, you see, is in the gift of Mr Brennan's company. One might almost say that it would have come from his own pocket. Such generosity in the cause of public welfare, with no regard for national boundaries, does him great credit, of course. I was proud that my own little field of research should have won his interest.

'At the same time I could not help feeling that a personal relationship was involved. I was bound to ask myself: Should I, on behalf of my company, accept this wonderful gift from this man? There seemed no reason why not. I made discreet inquiries. It soon became clear that here was a gentleman of considerable attainment. The firm he had helped to create was already prosperous, and promised to become immeasurably more so by the sale of its latest drug. As for Dr Erich Brunnen himself . . .'

Brennan crashed his fist on the cabinet by which he was standing. Jarred wineglasses sent forth an angry little carillon.

'This is quite unforgivable!' he shouted. 'It has nothing whatever to do with the inspector or anyone else. If you . . .'

Purbright raised a restraining hand. 'Come now, Mr Brennan. No one is challenging your right to travel under any name you wish. Celebrities do it all the time.

I cannot see that this lady has made anything in the nature of an accusation.'

'That is not the point,' Brennan retorted. 'You are letting her go on and on with all this irrelevant nonsense. Why should I put up with it? What the devil has my private or my professional life to do with an attack on some servant girl in this ridiculous little town of yours?'

The inspector looked at him thoughtfully. 'I don't recall,' he said, quietly, 'describing her as a servant girl.' He waited, then made a gesture of indifference, 'However, perhaps Miss Teatime will finish what she was telling us.'

Miss Teatime, who had been staring uncomfortably at the carpet, raised her head.

'I am sorry, but I had no intention of upsetting Dr Brunnen. I was simply going to say that what I learned about him was just as reassuring as the result of my inquiries about his firm. Long before his success in the drug industry, he had made quite a name in medical research at one of those big experimental institutes—what was it again?—Raven-something-or-other . . . Never mind, I must not embarrass him with a list of achievements. What really matters is that I decided it would be quite proper to accept the grant.

'And then, only two days ago, something happened that made me change my mind completely. Something absolutely unaccountable, and more distressing than I can say.'

She glanced timidly at the inspector. At the same time, one of her hands stole to the opposite shoulder and massaged it gently, as if to soothe the pain of a recent injury.

All three men were watching her, Brennan with as much bewilderment as anybody.

'It was in the surgery of poor Dr Meadow,' Miss Teatime resumed, seemingly with considerable reluctance. 'Both Dr Brunnen and I went into the consulting room immediately after his collapse. I do not think that Dr Brunnen knew I was just behind him. He cannot have known. For one of the first things he did—with that unfortunate man lying there dead on the floor—was to steal Dr Meadow's stethoscope and hide it away under his jacket.'

CHAPTER EIGHTEEN

A dead silence extended for fully five seconds before Brennan managed to push words past the blockage of his anger.

'But she's demented, this bloody woman! This, this . . . *Wahnsinnige* . . .'

'Just a moment, sir.'

Purbright turned to Miss Teatime.

'Are you quite certain about this?'

'Absolutely. I only wish I were not. I mean, it was such a petty thing to do. A doctor filching another doctor's stethoscope. . . .'

'You're out of your mind!' shouted Brennan.

'It was,' continued Miss Teatime, undeterred, 'the meanness of it that shocked me. Like stealing straw to make a brick. Of course, I resolved at once that I could not possibly accept the five thousand pounds unless Dr Brunnen could give a completely satisfactory explanation for his behaviour.'

'And can you, sir?' Purbright blandly inquired of Brennan.

'But this is sheer fantasy! Can't you see that? She has been pestering me. Sexually, you understand? And because I would have nothing to do with her, she makes these lunatic accusations.'

'Stealing,' said Purbright, 'is what we in this country term an indictable offence, sir. I have to explain that, because the legal distinction is important. Technically speaking, this lady has laid information against you, Mr, er, Dr Brunnen, and it is my duty to take it seriously.'

'But you can't! I have told you why she's talking all this nonsense.'

'At the moment, it is your word against hers that it *is* nonsense. You must appreciate that I have to satisfy myself whether there is any truth in Miss Teatime's charge. The other matter can wait for the time being.'

'What other matter?'

'The question of your whereabouts at eight o'clock on the evening of the twelfth.'

Brennan cast a quick look at Miss Teatime, but she remained in patient contemplation of the inspector's face.

'Have you any objection,' Purbright asked, 'to our making a search of your property, sir?'

'Of course I have. I object very strongly to the way I am being treated as a criminal. But if you want to waste your time looking for what is not here, by all means look. I need hardly say that this whole affair will be brought to the notice of your Foreign Ministry.'

'Very well, sir. If you will kindly remain where you are for a few minutes . . . Oh, and perhaps the lady would be good enough to wait outside in the corridor.'

Purbright and Love searched less astutely than Miss Teatime had done, but a good deal more industriously. Love, whose duties had afforded him a similar opportunity only once before in his life, found it highly enjoyable and determined to drag it out. More than once, Purbright had to point out to him that no degree of criminal ingenuity was likely to have succeeded in secreting a stethoscope within a stud box or submerging it in a bottle of after-shave lotion.

They finished at last, however, and the inspector presented himself to the cooler but still resentful Brennan.

'Would you mind coming down with us to the garage, sir?'

They walked in silence along the corridor, passing Miss Teatime at the first turn. She waited a moment, then followed quietly a few yards behind.

Brennan, invited by Purbright to walk ahead, led the two policemen into the roofed enclosure and stood beside the grey Hillman. He was quite calm now. As he handed the inspector a key, he made the slightest of bows.

Purbright opened the car door.

The two cases were in the same position, but the raincoat had been pushed into one of the compartments beneath the facia. Purbright drew it out and unrolled it. Holding it up, he shook it. Of the scarf, or whatever had been wrapped in the coat before, there was now no sign. He folded the coat and laid it on the seat.

Love was busy excavating and scrutinizing the contents of the boot. He found a foot pump, a tin box with a few small tools in it, a deflated beach ball, some rope, a folded canvas stool, a lemonade bottle half filled with a liquid which he decided, after careful sniffing, to be paraffin, and a much worn tyre.

By the time Love had loaded these back again, the inspector had completed his examination of the inside of the car and was about to open the smaller of the two cases with one of the pair of keys helpfully volunteered by Brennan.

The case contained, as he had guessed, a range of

small sample bottles and packs of capsules. All bore labels under the Elixon imprint.

Purbright locked it again, replaced it on the seat, and pulled forward the larger case.

Sergeant Love looked over the inspector's shoulder as the lid was raised.

He could not have put names to more than two or three of the things he saw revealed, but he knew that they were pieces of diagnostic equipment of a kind he had seen from time to time in surgeries and hospitals. He recognized an instrument for looking into ears. Another, a sort of barometer, was similar to one by which he once had had his very normal blood pressure measured. There were slim chrome torches, rubber-headed mallets, thermometers in transparent pocket cases, stainless steel spatulas. All were sealed in polythene and neatly arranged in compartments. Love gazed admiringly at their workmanship and pristine brightness. No wonder, he reflected, that it cost so much to set up as a doctor.

'Go on, inspector,' he heard Brennan say quietly. 'There's more under those.'

Purbright gave the top section a pull. It lifted and hinged back. He reached into the bottom of the case and drew up something black and tubular and flabby.

The sergeant very nearly said, 'Ah!'

Then Purbright's hand went again into the case.

Another stethoscope emerged.

Then another. And another.

By now, the inspector was looking rather like a man who had unwisely allowed himself to assist in some bizarre and protracted feat of conjuring.

Brennan, his face expressionless save for a slight thrusting forward of his lips that gave him something of a proprietory air, looked on.

The seventh, and final, stethoscope joined the bundle in Purbright's left hand. He stood up. Love gazed with open wonder at the collection.

Brennan smiled.

'And which one,' he asked, 'am I supposed to have stolen, inspector?'

It was a good question, Purbright bitterly reflected. Unless an answer presented itself pretty quickly, it was a winner.

He diligently examined the seven stethoscopes, comparing one with another. All seemed brand new and of exactly the same pattern. Their design, though, was unconventional—or so he supposed—for at the union of the earpieces was a small black box fitted with a rocker switch. A metal strip riveted to the top of this box carried the word Elixon in red.

'These are manufactured by your firm, are they, sir?'

'No, but they are made to our specification.'

'And you sell them?'

'I do not think you quite understand, inspector. All this'—he made general indication of the stethoscopes and the other contents of the case—'is just a small extra service that we are pleased to perform for the medical profession. Doctors find them very acceptable, I think.'

'You mean they're free gifts?'

Brennan received this interpretation coldly. 'They are gestures that help to maintain good will between one profession and another, that is all.'

'Rather expensive gestures,' Purbright remarked. He was looking closely at the stethoscope he had kept in his hand after dropping the others back in the case. 'I don't know much about these things, but this seems to be of fairly advanced design.'

'Oh, it is. This type is extremely sensitive. Electronics, of course.'

Brennan moved close. He held the black box lightly in his open palm.

'In here are the transistors, battery, and so forth. It is a very small radio set, in fact.' His fingers, the inspector noticed, bore several black grease smears. 'You simply press this switch and you can hear a heart making a noise like an ocean liner.'

Purbright gave the switch experimental pressure, but Brennan shook his head.

'No, no—it is designed to work only when the earpieces are extended in use. To prevent accidental battery wear, you see.'

'And what's this?' The inspector peered at the lettering he indicated with one finger immediately below the switch.

'*Verstärker*—amplifier,' Brennan explained.

For some time Purbright continued to stare at the tiny moulded letters. Then, without taking his eyes off them, he beckoned.

'Sergeant. . . .'

Love, who had been stooping to look under the car, stood upright and came to Purbright's side.

'Read that out loud, will you.' Purbright told him.

'Vurze . . .' He hesitated, and made a second attempt. 'Vurzetarker. . . .' He looked inquiringly at the inspector. 'Is that right?'

'It will do, sergeant. It will do very nicely.'

Love withdrew and resumed his painstaking scrutiny of the car's underbelly, watched impassively by Miss Teatime.

'Did Dr Meadow,' Purbright asked Brennan, 'possess one of these stethoscopes?'

'No. They are a completely new line. As a matter of

fact, I intended to give him one that day when he collapsed. If you remember, I was waiting to see him.'

'And you had it on you, did you?'

Brennan agreed, almost eagerly, that he had indeed been carrying the instrument intended for Dr Meadow.

'Of course!' he exclaimed. 'This lady must have noticed it sticking from my pocket and concluded that I had stolen it!'

'That could be the explanation, sir.'

'Could? It must be. Does a man with a case full of beautiful instruments like this steal an old stethoscope from some little country doctor?'

Purbright smilingly conceded that such behaviour was most unlikely. He was sorry that Mr Brennan—or Dr Brunnen, rather—had been subjected to inconvenience.

Brennan (or Brunnen) bowed. Not at all. These little misunderstandings did arise from time to time. He quite understood. Perhaps now that the matter had been cleared up, however . . .

In the midst of this mutual affability, Purbright had been keeping a wary eye on the progress of Sergeant Love. By now, he had methodically worked round to the front of the car and had just raised the lid of the engine compartment.

'Excuse me a moment, sir,' Purbright said to Brennan. 'We might as well finish the formalities.'

He casually walked over to join Love and leaned with him over the engine.

'If it's anywhere,' he murmured very softly, 'it's in here. He's still got oil on his hands.'

Both men peered intently into every recess, every conceivable hiding place from end to end of the engine compartment. Love probed beneath the cylinder block and behind the clutch housing and would have unscrewed both the radiator and oil filler caps had not Purbright dissuaded him.

The search revealed nothing.

Purbright was the first to straighten up. He took care not to sigh too obviously. The sergeant remained dutifully inclined over the engine for a few minutes more. Then he, too, stepped back.

Purbright looked towards Brennan.

'That appears to be all, then, sir,' he said. He motioned Love to close the lid.

'Excuse me, inspector.'

Purbright turned to find beside him the small figure of Miss Teatime. She was gazing pensively at the car.

'That model, if I remember rightly,' she said, 'is fired with a one-and-a-half litre engine.'

'I wouldn't know,' said Purbright, more abruptly than he had intended.

'A four-cylinder engine, in fact,' she said.

'Possibly.'

'No, inspector—quite definitely. So why, I wonder, should there appear to be six distributor leads? I thought I had better mention it before the sergeant puts the bonnet down.'

Purbright reached forward and parted the complex of black rubber-covered cables that ran from the distributor to the four sparking plugs. Two were loose. They had been tucked and twisted amongst the others. And now that he was deliberately looking at them and not simply glimpsing and accepting them as familiar parts of a car's mechanism, their greater thickness and newness registered immediately.

He tugged them free.

There came to light the little black box at their junction, then the stethoscope's third tube, the foot of the 'Y', ending in the button-like microphone housing.

Purbright examined the find. It appeared to be identical with the seven instruments in Brennan's case. The same design, the same workmanship, the same little Elixon name plate. Yet there was a difference. This one was noticeably heavier.

'Do you wish to give me any explanation about this, sir?'

Brennan stared contemptuously into the middle distance. He said nothing.

The inspector waited a while, then handed the stethoscope to Love and again addressed Brennan.

'Erich Brunnen, or Brennan, I am now going to take you into custody. You will be charged with stealing, at or about half past six in the evening of the twelfth of this month, in Heston Lane, Flaxborough, one stethoscope, the property of Dr Augustus Meadow . . .'

'What a fiendish device, Mr Purbright!'

It was three days later.

The Chief Constable was looking at a sketch that the inspector had made on the back of an envelope.

'Yes, sir. The forensic people were quite impressed. That, you see'—he pointed—'is the compressed air cartridge, rather like a soda syphon bulb, which releases its charge when that switch is pressed. Hence the hissing noise that Mrs McCreavy mistakenly ascribed to Dr Meadow's impatience.

'Now look at the two tubes that form the earpieces. That one is just a dummy, like the bottom tube with its imitation microphone, but the other is a piece of small-bore hydraulic hose with steel mesh reinforcement under a smooth rubber facing. A sort of flexible gun barrel, in fact.'

'Good Lord!' said Mr Chubb. 'I see what you're getting at, of course. The whole thing's a kind of air gun.'

'Exactly, sir. And pretty powerful, according to the lab report.'

'What does it fire? A pellet, or something?'

'No, sir. Probably a dart, a small steel spike. As you can imagine, it would have to be fairly sharp to pass through the petrous bone.'

'Yes, of course it would.' Mr Chubb saw no immediate reason to admit that he had never before heard of petrous bone.

'Tell me, Mr Purbright—why did you suppose this fellow to be lying when he claimed he had not seen Dr Meadow that day?'

'I knew for certain that he was lying as soon as I saw the word that was printed under the switch. The German word for amplifier—Verstärker. The last thing that Dr Meadow said before he collapsed was so curious that Mrs McCreavy remembered it. According to her, it was "The fur's darker". That is just how a muttered and probably anglicized pronunciation of the word would be interpreted by someone overhearing it. So it was clear that Meadow had been using one of Brennan's new stethoscopes. And there was only one way he could have got hold of it. Brennan must have presented him with it before the surgery opened at six o'clock.'

'I suppose that from then on Brennan was hanging around in order to reclaim the thing as soon as it had . . . well, gone off?'

'Yes, sir. It was essential to prevent its being examined by anybody else.'

'He was taking an awful risk, wasn't he?'

Purbright shrugged. 'There was a great deal at stake, sir. We've turned up a copy of the letter Meadow wrote to Elixon immediately after the inquest on Alderman Winge. It stated his misgivings about this drug "Juniform" and said that he would have to withdraw what he had published previously about its safety. Brennan and his firm stood to lose sales that promised eventually to be worth millions. Men in that position do tend to favour boldness.'

'Lucky that Teatime person had her wits about her, eh?' remarked Mr Chubb. 'We owe her quite a lot, you know.'

'Yes, sir. She seems a very public-spirited lady.'

Inspector Purbright, too, could be magnanimous when he wished.